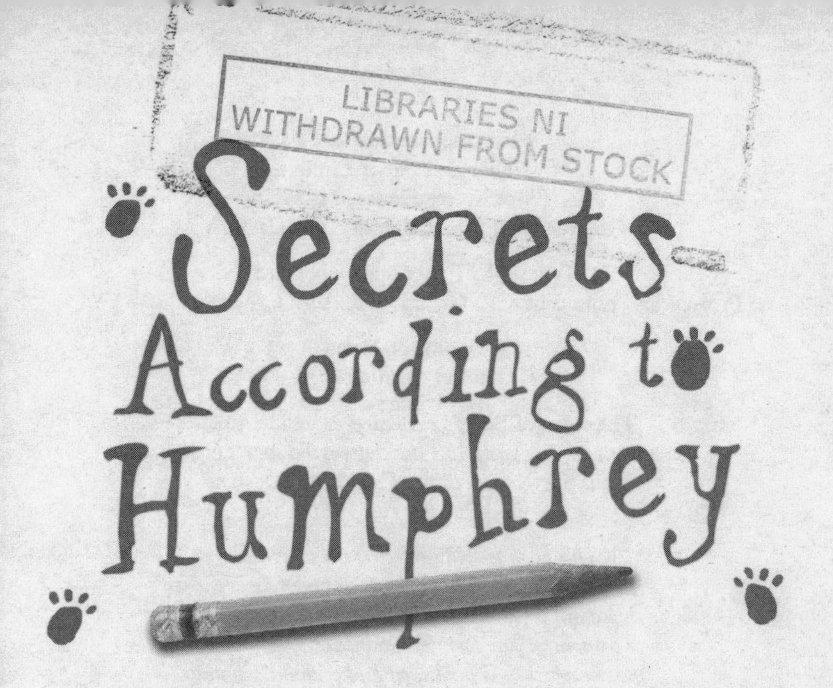

Betty G. Birney

FABER & FABER

First published in 2014
by Faber and Faber Limited
Bloomsbury House, 74–77
Great Russell Street, London WC1B 3DA

Typeset by Faber and Faber Ltd
Printed and bound by CPI Group (UK) Ltd, Croydon CR0 4YY

A CIP record for this book
is available from the British Library

ISBN 978-0-571-28249-4

2 4 6 8 10 9 7 5 3 1

To my granddaughter – and Humphrey's friend – Remy Bella Frank.

Thanks to Susan Patron for helping to guide Humphrey and me through the library!

Contents

1

Secrets of the Nile

If I've learned one thing in my job as a classroom hamster, it's that there is no such thing as an ordinary day at school. But the day the secrets started, I couldn't have guessed what was in store for us in Room 26.

The holidays were over and I was HAPPY-HAPPY-HAPPY to catch up on my sleep. I followed along with the morning lessons, but I also took time to get a little rest.

After my friends left for mid-morning break, I settled down in my nice, soft bedding and closed my eyes. When I opened them again, I was unsqueakably shocked to look up and see our teacher, Mrs Brisbane, writing our new vocabulary words on the board.

There was nothing strange about that.

But there was something very strange about what she was writing.

Instead of writing words like 'marsh', 'journey' and 'approach', our teacher was writing odd strings of letters that didn't look like any words I'd ever seen.

pharaoh
papyrus
pyramid
hieroglyphics

I think 'journey' is a difficult word to spell. But 'pharaoh' and 'hieroglyphics'? How can those letters work together at all?

Of course, Mrs Brisbane doesn't normally put nonsense words on the board.

Another thing I've learned in my classroom job is that just when you think you understand everything about how humans think and act, you learn something completely new.

Since I was the only one there to notice what was happening and I am a good classroom hamster, I felt I had to squeak up.

'Mrs Brisbane? Are you sure those are words?' I asked.

All right, I know that all she heard was SQUEAK-SQUEAK-SQUEAK, but I wanted to make my point.

'Quiet, Humphrey,' Mrs Brisbane said. 'You'll find out what's happening soon enough.'

'BOING-BOING!' my neighbour Og commented.

He lives in a tank right next to my cage.

He makes a strange sound like a broken guitar string, because he's a strange frog.

I don't speak frog, but I think he was as confused as I was.

'Og, what is she doing?' I squeaked to him.

'BOING-BOING-BOING!' He leaped into the water and made a lot of loud splashing sounds.

Mrs Brisbane stopped writing and looked in our direction.

'Sometimes, I think you two actually understand everything that's going on in Room Twenty-six.' She chuckled and went on writing.

'Of course we do!' I replied. 'We're your

classroom pets! We know everything that's going on – except what you are doing right now.'

Og splashed and splashed and splashed some more, while I hopped on my wheel and went for a spin.

When I'm worried or excited, spinning helps me think.

Soon, my friends all returned to Room 26.

After they'd hung up their coats and put away their hats and gloves and scarves, they were back in their seats and looking at the board.

Slow-Down-Simon's hand went up right away.

'Mrs Brisbane, are we supposed to learn those words?' he asked. 'Because they look really hard!'

'YES-YES-YES!' I agreed, but Mrs Brisbane just smiled and nodded.

'Yes, they are, class, but you're going to be learning a lot about these words in the next few weeks,' she explained. 'Now, what do you think we're going to be studying?'

Small-Paul raised his hand. (We have two boys named Paul in our class. Since Paul F. is shorter than Paul G., I call him Small-Paul.)

'Something to do with Egypt?' he answered when Mrs Brisbane called on him.

'Yes!' Mrs Brisbane said. 'We're going to be studying ancient Egypt.'

Then she added the words 'ancient' and 'Egypt' to the list on the board.

Most of my classmates looked excited, but I have to admit I still had no idea what Mrs Brisbane meant.

'What other words can I write on the board to go along with these?' she asked.

'I know!' Be-Careful-Kelsey waved her hand. 'Mummy!'

Mrs Brisbane added the word to the board.

Now, I know what a mummy is. I know what a daddy is, too. But I still didn't know anything about ancient Egypt.

Tell-the-Truth-Thomas waved his hand high in the air and Mrs Brisbane called on him.

'I read this book where a mummy came back to life and escaped from its tomb,' he said. 'It was a great book!'

I felt a shiver and a quiver but some of my friends said, 'Ooh' and 'Ahh!'

Thomas continued. 'Then, I read a true book about the pyramids and that King Toot!'

All my classmates giggled.

'I mean King Tut!' Thomas looked very pleased with himself. 'He was a pharaoh, which is like a king.'

'King . . . Tut?' I repeated. Because I know what a king is – sort of – but what's a tut?

'Very good, Thomas,' Mrs Brisbane said. 'You know quite a bit about ancient Egypt already.'

But she didn't write 'King Tut' on the board. Instead she wrote another string of nonsense letters: *Tutankhamen*.

'Tutankhamen was only a boy when he became a pharaoh. In the 1920s, his tomb was discovered and it was full of beautiful treasures,' Mrs Brisbane explained.

'I'm surprised she could figure out how to say that word,' I squeaked to my neighbour. 'Do you know what she's talking about?'

'BOING-BOING!' Og replied.

At least I wasn't the only one in the dark.

'To start our Egypt unit, we're going to the library now. Mr Fitch will be showing us a film that shows some of the wonders of King Tut's tomb. It's called *Secrets of the Nile.*'

She wrote 'Nile' on the board.

I had no idea what that meant, either, but at least it was short and easy to spell.

Soon, my fellow students lined up to go to the library.

'Can Humphrey come, too?' Rolling-Rosie asked as she rolled her wheelchair past my cage.

'Thanks, Rosie!' I squeaked.

My hopes were dashed when Mrs Brisbane said, 'I think Humphrey would probably rather take a little nap.'

But I wasn't the least bit tired!

On their way out of the room, I heard Simon ask Thomas what the name of the mummy book was.

'I can't remember,' Thomas said. 'I'll show it to you in the library.'

'Great, because I want to check it out,' Simon said.

'I want to learn those secrets of the Nile,' Rosie said as she rolled her wheelchair out the door.

'I want to see King Tut's treasure,' Holly said.

Before I knew it, Og and I were all alone in the room.

'Og, I want to know the secrets of the Nile, too, don't you?' I squeaked.

'BOING-BOING-BOING!' my friend replied.

'Whatever the Nile is,' I added.

I scurried over to the corner of my cage. There's a mirror there and behind the mirror is a secret: my tiny notebook and pencil that Ms Mac gave me.

I started to write down all of the weird words. I have to say, my paw was aching by the time I got to 'hieroglyphics'. It was the longest, strangest word I'd ever seen.

I tucked my notebook back into its hiding place just seconds before my friends returned, full of energy.

'Hi, Humphrey,' Stop-Talking-Sophie said as she passed by my cage. 'You should have seen what was in that pyramid. There was a—'

She didn't finish because just then Slow-Down-Simon tapped her on the shoulder and said, 'Don't tell Humphrey! They're supposed to be *secrets*!'

'I guess he wouldn't understand anyway,' she said.

'Yes, I would!' I squeaked. 'Please tell me! I'm in your class, too.'

Sophie smiled and said, 'Sorry, Humphrey. I can't tell you.'

Then Tall-Paul staggered to his seat with his arms up and said, 'I want my mummy!'

Everybody giggled.

Everybody except Og . . . and me.

I HOPED-HOPED-HOPED that Mrs Brisbane would talk about those secrets after lunch, but she moved on to other subjects instead.

Just before the bell rang at the end of the day, she had Helpful-Holly hand out the homework sheets.

'Class, as you'll see on the instructions, you need to unscramble the words and label some of the items we learned about today,' she said.

'When is it due?' Do-It-Now-Daniel asked.

'Tomorrow, Daniel,' Mrs Brisbane said. 'You'll have to do it tonight.'

Daniel sighed.

He liked to put things off as long as possible, if he could.

It only took a few moments for the room to empty after the bell rang.

Mrs Brisbane tidied her desk, as usual.

'Can you tell us about the secrets of the Nile?' I squeaked.

'What's that, Humphrey? Are you interested in ancient Egypt?' she asked.

'YES-YES-YES!' I answered.

'As if you know what I'm saying,' she said with a chuckle. 'Well, you'll find out what's going on soon enough.'

'But I'd like to know *now*!' I squeaked.

'BOING-BOING!' Og agreed.

'I might as well put the map up before I go,' she said.

She took a large, rolled-up paper from the cupboard and then tacked it to the noticeboard.

'There's ancient Egypt and there's the Nile.' She pointed at the map. 'You two will have to wait to learn the rest.'

Just then, the door opened and Mr Morales came in. He's the headmaster and the Most Important Person at Longfellow School.

'I'm glad you're still here, Sue,' he said.

Our teacher's first name is Sue, but I *always* call her Mrs Brisbane.

'I have some bad news,' Mr Morales said. 'And I have some good news, as well.'

'What's the bad news?' Mrs Brisbane asked.

'You're going to be losing one of your students in a few weeks,' he told her.

'Oh, no!' she replied. 'Who?'

'NO-NO-NO!' I shouted as I scrambled up to the top of my cage for a better look. 'WHO-WHO-WHO?'

To my surprise, Mr Morales smiled. 'This letter will explain. This is the good news,' he said as he handed Mrs Brisbane a piece of paper.

She read it and smiled. 'This is wonderful! I couldn't be happier,' she said.

Happy? Happy to be losing one of my classmates? I like every single one of my friends and I thought Mrs Brisbane did, too.

'As you can see, we want to keep the whole thing secret. No one else should know until the big day,' he said.

'I agree,' she said. 'I won't tell a soul. Oh, but can I tell Bert?'

Bert is Mr Brisbane's first name.

'Yes, but only Bert,' he said.

Og splashed around in his tank.

'What about us?' I squeaked.

'What about Humphrey and Og?' Mrs Brisbane asked Mr Morales.

The head looked our way and laughed. 'No, not even Humphrey and Og.'

And I thought Mr Morales liked us!

Soon, he was gone.

I crossed my toes and hoped Mrs Brisbane would leave the letter on her desk so I could read it later that night. But as she was gathering up papers to take home, she put the piece of paper in her handbag.

'NO-NO-NO!!!' I squeaked at the top of my small lungs.

'BOING!!!!!' Og twanged as he splashed around in the water side of his tank.

I guess she didn't hear us, because she said good night and closed the door behind her.

When the car park was empty (I can see it from my window), I jiggled the lock-that-doesn't-lock on my cage and it opened. Thank goodness I have a secret way of getting out of my cage!

I scampered over to Og's tank. 'Someone's leaving!' I said.

'BOING-BOING-BOING!' He sounded unsqueakably upset.

'Who could it be?' I asked.

Og didn't answer. He just stared straight ahead.

He has a very wide mouth that usually looks like a smile, but that night, he wasn't smiling at all.

He was the saddest frog I've ever seen.

(Yes, he's the only frog I've ever seen up close, but he did look sad.)

'What can we do?' I asked.

Og just sat there, as still and silent as the rock he was sitting on.

After a while, I went back to my cage and closed the door behind me.

Then I took out my notebook and began to write.

'Secrets can be VERY-VERY-VERY bad,' I wrote.

And I meant every single 'very'.

Humphrey's Top Secret Scribbles

There's just one thing I want to know:
Which of my friends is about to go?

More and More Secrets

'The Nile?' Aldo looked up at the map when he came into Room 26 to clean that night. 'You must be studying Egypt.'

'YES-YES-YES!' I squeaked. 'Can you tell us more about it?'

Aldo didn't answer.

Instead, he went right to work, sweeping the floor the way he does every night during the school week.

After a while, he said, 'Pyramids.'

'That's on our word list!' I shouted.

'Pharaohs,' he added. 'Mummies. King Tut.'

'That's right!' I agreed. 'Tell me more!'

Aldo stopped sweeping and leaned on his broom. 'I wonder if I'll ever get to see the

Nile River,' he said with a faraway look in his eyes.

So the Nile was a river! I had finally learned something about Egypt.

'BOING-BOING-BOING!' Og twanged.

Frogs like watery things more than hamsters, I guess.

'I'd like to teach students about Egypt someday,' he said.

I scrambled up to the highest point on the tree branch in my cage. 'You will!' I squeaked.

'Humphrey, now that I'm getting closer to finishing school, I can hardly wait until I can start teaching,' he said.

Aldo cleaned at Longfellow School at night. But during the day, he went to school so he could become a teacher, like Mrs Brisbane.

Well, maybe not exactly like Mrs Brisbane. After all, Aldo has a nice, big moustache and Mrs Brisbane doesn't!

Still, I think he'd make as good a teacher as she is.

Aldo got out a brown paper bag and pulled a chair up close to my cage and Og's tank.

'Let's see what Maria packed for me,' he said

as he opened the bag. 'Oh, a cheese sandwich, an apple and . . . I think maybe this is for you, Humphrey,' he said.

Aldo pulled a carrot stick out of his bag and pushed it through the bars of my cage.

'Thanks, Aldo! And thanks to Maria, too!' I squeaked.

I didn't eat all of the carrot stick right away. I hid some of it in my cheek pouch, which is a handy way for hamsters to store food. I also slipped part of it in my bedding for a lovely midnight snack.

Aldo ate part of his sandwich. Then he said, 'You know, Humphrey and Og, Maria's going to have a baby.'

I DID know that. 'Yes, that's GREAT-GREAT-GREAT!' I told him.

'BOING-BOING-BOING!' Og agreed.

'Thanks, guys. I'm a little nervous about being a dad. And I have some news—' Suddenly he stopped.

'What news?' I asked.

Og splashed noisily in his tank.

'Well, I want to tell you, but I can't,' Aldo said. 'It's a secret.'

Another secret? I was beginning to dislike secrets a lot!

'I mean, Maria told me not to tell anybody yet,' Aldo continued. 'It's a pretty big secret.'

'Tell us, Aldo,' I said. 'We're your friends. We won't tell anybody.'

Aldo pushed the uneaten part of his sandwich back into the bag. 'I know it's silly. Who would you tell?' he said. 'Still, I promised Maria I'd keep it a secret, so I will.'

I was feeling a little upset with Aldo. After all, if I told his secret to my friends in Room 26, all that they'd hear would be 'SQUEAK-SQUEAK-SQUEAK.'

Still, I guess a secret is a secret. And a promise is a promise.

I hopped on my wheel and began to spin.

'Sorry, Humphrey,' Aldo said. 'I'll tell you as soon as I can.'

My wheel was spinning like crazy, so I didn't even answer.

'BOING-BOING,' Og twanged.

He sounded as curious as I felt.

Soon, Aldo left Room 26 and turned out the lights.

I kept quiet until I saw his car pull out of the car park.

'What do you think Aldo's secret *is*?' I called to Og. 'And which student is leaving?'

Og splashed around and didn't answer.

'And what are the secrets of the Nile?' I asked.

I knew better than to expect an answer from Og.

Then I remembered the film that my classmates had seen earlier in the day.

I had a long night ahead of me, so I decided to take a little trip to the library. If I couldn't find out who was leaving our class, maybe I could at least learn some more things about Egypt.

As usual, I jiggled the lock-that-doesn't-lock, slid down the leg of my table and scampered across the floor to the door.

'I'll tell you everything when I get back, Og!' I squeaked just before I scrunched down and slid under the door.

It's a narrow gap, and I was HAPPY-HAPPY-HAPPY to get through to the other side.

From the sound of Og splashing in his tank,

I think he was happy, too.

At night, only the dimmest lights are on in the halls of Longfellow School, and it's unsqueakably quiet. But I knew the way to the library, so I hurried as fast as I could.

It's a tight squeeze under the door – EEEK! – but I made it. There I was, in the library with its shelves and shelves of books and its big glowing fish tank.

During the day, the fish tank probably wasn't eerie at all. But at night, the water is a ghostly blue.

There are brightly coloured fish bobbing in the water and lots of bubbles. And then there's the little sunken ship, lying at the bottom of the tank.

I didn't like to look at the sunken ship. *I* was in a boat once and it almost sank!

'Hi, guys,' I squeaked to the fish. 'It's me, Humphrey from Room Twenty-six. Hope you don't mind me dropping in!'

They didn't answer, of course, but their mouths moved. Were they trying to tell me something?

I can't imagine what it's like to be a fish and

live in the water all the time.

Just thinking about it makes me feel all shivery.

But I wasn't in the library to see the fish. I was in the library to learn about the secrets of the Nile.

I needed to get to the big table, so I scurried over to a series of shelves next to it.

The shelves were like steps and I climbed UP-UP-UP until I reached the top.

I remembered from an earlier visit that there was a big, bumpy remote control on the desk with buttons. If I pushed the right buttons, the big screen in the front of the room lit up.

Whew – it was still there. As soon as I pushed the top button, the big screen lit up brightly.

YES-YES-YES!

The words 'The End' came up on the screen and stayed there.

NO-NO-NO!

I didn't want to see the end until I'd seen the beginning and the middle!

The remote control had lots of buttons in different colours, with arrows going in every direction. And when I pushed the arrow that pointed this way ←, the picture started to move – backwards!

It went unsqueakably fast, so I could hardly tell what I was seeing.

There were people riding camels and lots of sand and a strip of water that must have been the Nile River.

There were some odd-looking buildings, too.

Finally, the picture stopped moving.

Then I pushed the middle button that said 'Play'.

'*Secrets of the Nile*,' a deep voice said.

I hunkered down on the desk and watched in amazement. Soon I'd know the secrets of the Nile, just like my friends did!

And oh, what I saw was pawsitively amazing.

Egypt is a country in Africa, located on the Nile River – the longest river in the whole wide world! It runs through ten countries and not only that – there is a White Nile and a Blue Nile.

Ancient Egypt was quite a place.

Thousands of years ago the Egyptians built gigantic pyramids, which are buildings shaped like big triangles, in honour of their kings. The kings were called *pharaohs*. (Pharaoh rhymes with 'aero', like in 'aeroplane'.)

The pyramids held a secret – there was treasure inside. Lots and lots of treasure!

But there were also mummies, which were bodies all wrapped up from head to toe.

'EEEK!' I squeaked when I saw pictures of them. These mummies were not like mothers or fathers or anything I'd seen!

That's not all. There was also a strange-looking statue of a very odd creature. It had a body like a huge lion, but the head was like a human!

This was a *Sphinx*. (Which rhymes with 'inks', 'pinks' and 'winks'.)

The voice said that in ancient Greece, they also had a legend about a Sphinx.

The Sphinx guarded a city. When a traveller wanted to enter the city, the Sphinx asked him a riddle. If the stranger didn't know the answer, then he couldn't come in – or worse!

By the time the words 'The End' came up again, my tail was twitching, my whiskers were wiggling and my fur was standing up on end.

I hit the top button on the remote control and the screen went black.

I scurried down the shelves, slid under the door a little more easily and RAN-RAN-RAN through the halls of Longfellow School.

Believe me, I was happy to get back to Room 26, where there were no mummies or pyramids and not one single Sphinx.

Of course, there was a frog waiting to hear all about my adventure. He greeted me with a 'BOING-BOING-BOING!'

I scurried across the room, grabbed the cord of the blinds and swung myself back up to the table.

By the time I got to Og's tank, I was out of breath.

'Og!' I panted. 'Desert, treasure, Sphinx, a riddle! And a mummy is *not* somebody's mother!'

My froggy friend splashed loudly. 'BOING-BOING-BOING!'

I guess frogs don't like the desert, where it's very dry.

I yawned. 'I'll explain it all tomorrow.'

I was unsqueakably tired and the sky was getting light outside. So I hurried over to my cage and was very happy to close the door behind me.

I checked to make sure that the lock-that-doesn't-lock was fastened tightly.

Then I dived under my soft, warm bedding and fell asleep right away.

Humans might think that hamsters don't dream, but they'd be wrong.

In my dream that night, I rode a camel with a huge hump across the desert, past the pyramids and right up to the gigantic Sphinx.

And you know what? It *talked* to me!

'Tell me your secrets,' the Sphinx said in a ghostly voice. 'And I'll tell you mine.'

'But I don't have any secrets,' I squeaked to him.

'Then you cannot pass,' the Sphinx said. 'You will stay here in the desert . . . for ever!'

And then *he* or *she* or *it* laughed.

It laughed so hard, I woke up – thank goodness.

It was almost time for school to start, so I decided it would be better to stay awake than to stay in ancient Egypt with the Sphinx for ever.

I grabbed my notebook from behind the mirror and began to write down all the secrets I'd learned so far.

Humphrey's Top Secret Scribbles

Just thinking about meeting up with a
mummy
Makes me feel funny in my tummy.

Secret Guest

Even if I'd wanted to forget about ancient Egypt for a while, I couldn't. Everything we did in Room 26 had something to do with that subject!

Mrs Brisbane divided the class into four groups: the Scribes (those were people who wrote things down), the Builders, the Traders and the Artists. Each group was assigned to study one part of Egyptian life and do a project and a report on the subject.

'What group would you want to be in?' I squeaked to Og during break.

He splished and splashed.

'You like water,' I said. 'I guess you'd like to be a Trader so you could travel up and down the Nile.'

It wasn't easy for me to figure out what I'd like to be.

I like writing in my notebook, so it would be fun to be a Scribe.

Scribes wrote with a strange alphabet using little pictures instead of letters. They're called *hieroglyphs*, a word that is pronounced *hire-oh-glifs* and doesn't rhyme with anything.

On the other paw, it would be fun to be a Builder and make a model pyramid.

The Traders were going to have a GREAT-GREAT-GREAT time building a model boat and learning how ancient Egyptians traded.

Oh, but the Artists would get to make all kinds of beautiful pots, jars and statues and decorate them.

Luckily, as classroom pets, Og and I got to see what all the groups were doing.

But as I watched them huddling together in their groups, travelling back and forth to the library and laughing, I suddenly remembered that one of my classmates would soon be leaving!

And when she'd heard about it, Mrs Brisbane had said she couldn't be happier.

I'd be sad if any one of them left.

I'd miss watching Helpful-Holly pass out homework and the big smile on Forgetful-Phoebe's face when she remembered hers.

I'd miss Rolling-Rosie popping wheelies in her wheelchair and the way Just-Joey likes to talk with me alone.

Class would be duller without Calm-Down-Cassie and the way she blurts out, 'Oh, no!' whenever something unexpected happens.

How could Small-Paul get along without his best friend, Tall-Paul? Or the other way round?

I'd certainly miss Fix-It-Felipe, who always knows how to fix a torn page or prop up a wobbly chair leg. (Although I worry that someday he'll also fix my lock-that-doesn't-lock.)

Room 26 would be sad if anyone stopped coming every day. There wasn't one student in Room 26 that I wouldn't miss.

And I hoped that there wasn't one student in Room 26 who wouldn't miss me!

(Og, too, of course!)

So, as the week went on, I watched my friends working in their groups and wondered which one would be going – and how my life and the lives of all my friends would change.

On Friday, Mrs Brisbane said, 'I can't remember who's taking Humphrey home for the weekend.'

Phoebe's hand shot up so fast, it was a blur.

'I am!' she shouted. 'It's my turn!'

She was happy and so was I!

Phoebe Pratt lived with her grandmother, Mrs Lawson, while her parents were in a faraway country. I'd met her grandmother, who was an unsqueakably nice human. I was pretty sure I'd have a great weekend, unless Phoebe happened to have a large, fierce animal, such as a dog or a cat.

'Humphrey, I hope you know how special you are,' Mrs Lawson said when she came to pick us up after school. 'My boss actually let me leave work early to pick you up.'

'THANKS-THANKS-THANKS,' I squeaked.

'See, Gran, he talks,' Phoebe explained.

Gran laughed. 'If you say so, Phoebe.'

'BOING!' Og chimed in.

'May we take Og home, too?' Phoebe asked.

'I'm afraid it's too cold to take him outside

to the car,' Mrs Brisbane said. 'He doesn't have a fur coat like Humphrey.'

'BOING-BOING.' Og dived into the water side of his tank and began to swim.

'Sorry, Og,' I said.

Mrs Lawson covered my cage with a small blanket and picked it up.

'Stay warm this weekend, Og!' I squeaked. 'Bye!'

I'm not sure he heard me through the blanket.

Phoebe and her grandmother lived in a flat, so we had to go up in a lift. We got to the fifth floor so fast, I felt like my tummy was left on the ground floor!

'Where do you want him?' Gran asked.

'My room, of course!' Phoebe said. 'Right on my desk.'

I was happy to find out that Phoebe and her grandmother did not have any large animals roaming around the house.

And I was so pleased to see a big smile on Phoebe's face. In fact, I'd never seen her so happy.

'Wait until I tell my mum and dad I have you

home for the weekend,' she said. 'I wish they could meet you.'

Suddenly, Phoebe didn't look so happy.

I knew how much she missed her parents, and how FAR-FAR-FAR away they were. So I did everything I could think of to cheer her up.

First, I climbed up the side of my cage and leaped to my tree branch.

Phoebe giggled. 'Go, Humphrey,' she said.

Next, I swung from branch to branch to branch.

'Go, Humphrey, go!' Phoebe was grinning again.

Then, I dropped down into my bedding and did a triple somersault.

Phoebe laughed out loud.

Finally, I hopped on my wheel and spun it as fast as I could.

'Way to go, Humphrey!' She clapped her hands.

I kept on spinning, feeling unsqueakably happy to see Phoebe smiling again.

'Did I hear giggling?' Gran popped her head in the door.

'Humphrey's so funny,' Phoebe said. 'Watch.'

Mrs Lawson came in close to the cage.

I couldn't let Phoebe down, so this time, I scrambled up to the tippy top of my cage and made my way from one side to the other, paw over paw.

'He's very strong,' Gran said.

Then I let one paw go and held on with the other paw.

'Oh, my!' Gran said.

Next, I dropped down on to my tree branch and scrambled DOWN-DOWN-DOWN.

'Wow!' Gran exclaimed.

Again, I ended up on the wheel, spinning as fast as my small hamster legs could go.

'You're right, Phoebe,' Gran said. 'He really knows how to put on a show.'

I was pleased that Phoebe and her grandmother were impressed, but I wasn't sure I had enough energy to keep them smiling all weekend!

'I was going to ask if you wanted to see a movie, but Humphrey's much more entertaining,' Gran said.

'Gran, could I invite someone over?' Phoebe asked.

'Sure. Who do you want to ask?' her grandmother replied.

Phoebe glanced at my cage and giggled.

'I'll tell you in the kitchen,' she said. 'It's a secret.'

'Tell *me*!' I squeaked. 'Please!'

But they'd already left the room.

There was nothing to do but wait, so I crawled into my sleeping hut and closed my eyes.

I didn't open them again until Phoebe raced back in.

'She's coming tomorrow, Humphrey! Surprise!' she said.

'WHO-WHO-WHO?' I asked.

'You'll see,' Phoebe answered. 'Just wait.'

Surprises can be a lot of fun.

But what if the surprise was something like a dog or a cat?

I didn't have much choice, so I waited.

The surprise was Kelsey Kirkpatrick.

I call her Be-Careful-Kelsey because she doesn't always think before she does something.

'Look before you leap,' Mrs Brisbane sometimes says.

Kelsey tends to leap and not look at all, but she's been working on being a lot more careful.

Kelsey has long legs and bright red hair, and when she raced into Phoebe's room, she said, 'Hi, Humphrey! Surprised to see me?'

'Yes,' I said. 'And it's an unsqueakably good surprise.'

'I was hoping we could go to the zoo,' Gran told the girls. 'But it's pouring rain out there. I'm sure you'll think up something to do.'

I've heard about the zoo. There are animals even larger and more ferocious than dogs and cats.

I shivered just thinking about that place! I was GLAD-GLAD-GLAD that we weren't going there!

The girls spent most of the day in Phoebe's room, which was great for me.

It didn't take long before they were talking about ancient Egypt.

'What are the Builders doing?' Phoebe asked.

Kelsey giggled. 'We're building a pyramid. It's going to be *huge*. What about the Scribes?'

'We're inventing our own hieroglyphs,' Phoebe said. 'And we're going to make papyrus, like the Egyptians did. It's like handmade paper.'

'Pa-pie-rus?' I repeated. 'Is it made of pie?'

Both girls giggled.

'I think Humphrey wants to be a Scribe, too,' Phoebe said. 'He needs some papyrus.'

I already am a scribe and I don't need papyrus, because I have my little notebook. Of course, Phoebe and Kelsey don't know about *that*.

'Papyrus is made of reeds, but we're using strips of paper,' Phoebe continued.

'You're making paper out of paper?' I squeaked, but of course, she didn't understand me.

'And we're going to write something using

our special alphabet,' Phoebe said, and then added, 'I'd like to go to Egypt and see the pyramids. And ride a camel!'

'Eeek!' I said. Camels looked unsqueakably fearsome, especially when they show their teeth. Not only that, they *spit*. How rude is that?

'I'd like to go to New York City,' Kelsey said. 'My dad says he wants to take the whole family there.'

New York City has TALL-TALL-TALL buildings, but I don't think they have a lot of camels.

'You know what we could do?' Phoebe said. 'Pretend to live in ancient Egypt.'

Kelsey looked excited. 'Let's dress up like mummies! We could wrap ourselves in toilet paper!'

'Let's ask Gran,' Phoebe said.

The girls ran out of the room.

I was GLAD-GLAD-GLAD to see Phoebe so happy.

But I HOPED-HOPED-HOPED that she and Kelsey wouldn't wrap me in toilet paper.

I scurried into my sleeping hut, just in case.

Humphrey's Top Secret Scribbles

A camel's interesting to see,
But keep it far away from me!

4

Unsqueakable Secrets

I must have dozed off for a while, but I woke up when Phoebe and Kelsey raced back into the room, laughing.

'Humphrey! Where are you?' Kelsey peeked in my cage.

I poked my head out of the bedding.

'Here!' I squeaked.

'Gran didn't think we should waste a whole roll of toilet paper, so she cut an old sheet into strips,' Phoebe said. 'It will make us even better mummies!'

I darted under my bedding again and dozed for a bit. Sometimes I heard laughing, but I didn't look out. I didn't want the girls to think about wrapping bits of cloth around me. I don't like to wear anything except my fur coat.

'Ooh, that tickles.' Phoebe giggled.

'I can't see!' Kelsey shouted.

Then Phoebe said, 'Look in the mirror!'

They howled with laughter.

I must admit, I was getting curious about what was so funny.

After a while, Kelsey shrieked, 'Humphrey! Look at us!'

I couldn't resist. I popped my head up and looked.

'The Mummies!' the girls shouted.

'Eeek!' I squeaked.

Phoebe and Kelsey stood in front of my cage, almost completely wrapped in strips of white cloth.

All I could see was a little bit of their eyes and mouths.

They looked like the mummies in *Secrets of the Nile*!

'Mummy girls, mummy girls! We are the mummy girls!' Phoebe and Kelsey chanted.

They began to do a dance, hopping around the room and waving their arms.

I climbed up on my tree branch for a better

look. Believe me, it was quite a sight to see.

'Do you like our mummy dance, Humphrey?' Phoebe asked.

'YES-YES-YES!' I said.

Gran came into the room to see what all the noise was about and laughed when she saw the dancing mummies. She got her camera and took photos to show Phoebe's parents.

'Don't you want to be a mummy, Gran?' Phoebe asked.

'No,' Gran answered with a chuckle. 'I want to be a *grand-mummy*! But aren't you two hungry?'

'Starving!' Phoebe answered.

'Me too,' Kelsey said. 'But it's going to be kind of hard to eat.'

I guess *real* mummies don't eat much!

The girls decided to take off the strips of cloth.

It was taking a long time until Kelsey said, 'I know a faster way.'

She took one end of Phoebe's cloth and had her friend whirl around and around in a circle. As she twirled, the cloth unwound.

Then Kelsey twirled out of her cloth until she looked like herself again.

'Now, let's eat!' Phoebe said and the girls raced out of the room.

I was hungry from watching the dancing mummies. Luckily, I had some food stored in my cheek pouch – yum! (We hamsters make sure we never go hungry!)

Phoebe and Kelsey were still giggling when they returned from lunch.

'What now?' Phoebe flopped on to her bed.

'I don't know. What other Egyptian things could we do?' Kelsey dropped on to the chair.

The girls thought for a while.

'We could be scribes,' Phoebe said. 'We could make up an alphabet of pictures.'

Kelsey jumped up. 'Ooh – I know!' Her cheeks were pink with excitement. 'We could make an alphabet that only the two of us know. Then we could send each other messages.'

'Like a secret code!' Phoebe exclaimed.

'Sounds unsqueakably fun!' I agreed.

'Humphrey, why are you squeaking? Hamsters can't read,' Kelsey said.

'Well, *I* can read!' I was a tiny bit annoyed. I hopped on my wheel and began to SPIN-SPIN-SPIN.

Phoebe and Kelsey didn't even notice as they sat side by side on Phoebe's bed with paper and pencils.

'We need to come up with pictures that stand for sounds,' Kelsey said.

'Why don't we replace the letters of the alphabet? Like a square for A, a star for B – simple things that aren't too hard to draw,' Phoebe suggested.

I was getting tired of spinning and I didn't like feeling left out, so I went in my little sleeping hut for a nap.

When I woke up, I heard Phoebe and Kelsey talking. I strolled out of my little house, over to the side of the cage near the bed.

'Okay, so now we have our secret alphabet,' Kelsey said. 'What are we going to write?'

'I know,' Phoebe said. 'But don't tell Humphrey!'

She whispered in Kelsey's ear. They huddled together and kept whispering as they wrote.

Once, Kelsey said, 'No, not a star – it's a circle.'

Then Phoebe said, 'That arrow points the wrong way.'

There I was, watching two of my favourite

friends sharing a secret . . . without me.

I guess Forgetful-Phoebe forgot about me.

And Be-Careful-Kelsey wasn't being careful not to hurt my feelings.

'Who'd like to get out of this room and watch a video? I'll make popcorn,' Gran said as she opened the door again.

'I would,' Phoebe said.

'Count me in' Kelsey agreed.

Yum – popcorn sounded crunchy and delicious.

'Me too,' I added.

But the girls raced out of the room – without me.

'Wait!' I squeaked, but they didn't come back.

I sat and stared at the door for a while, hoping someone would remember that I like videos and popcorn, too.

After a while, I got tired of that and looked at the desk.

Then I saw it: right there near my cage. The girls had left the papers with the secret alphabet and the note they wrote.

And even though they said the alphabet was a secret, I was unsqueakably curious.

When I've visited other friends, I've noticed that movies are pretty long, so, I decided to take a chance.

I jiggled the lock-that-doesn't-lock and scurried over to the papers.

One piece had a list of letters and strange shapes and squiggles.

'This doesn't make sense!' I squeaked.

A = □
B = ☆
C = +
D = #
E = ▼
F = $
G = ✧
H = ➢
I = ✳
J = ●
K = ▲
L = 〰
M = ∽
N = ?
O = ∞
P = 👁
Q = ↨
R = ×
S = ♥
T = ¢
U = ■
V = ✔
W = ◗
X = ⁚
Y = ⟪
Z = ⟹

The other piece of paper had a series of symbols:

◗▼ ~∞✔▼ ➢■~👁 ➢×▼《

My whiskers wiggled and my tail twitched. This was harder than any maths problem I'd ever seen!

I was about to run back into my cage and close the door behind me, when I noticed that on the alphabet page there was a ◗ next to the W. And a ▼ next to the E.

W. E. Could the word be 'We?'

If I matched the symbols on the second sheet of paper with the ones next to the alphabet, maybe I could figure out the words.

It was hard work for a small hamster to crawl up and down a big piece of paper to work out what each letter meant.

I had gotten this far: 'WE LOVE HUMPH,' when I noticed that it was getting dark outside.

The girls might be coming back any minute!

I hurried into my cage and pulled the door behind me, making sure that it was tightly closed.

I was feeling a lot better as I remembered what I'd read.

Even though I hadn't reached the end, I was

pretty sure their secret message said, 'WE LOVE HUMPHREY.'

How could I have thought they didn't care?

My whiskers wiggled with joy.

Phoebe and Kelsey burst back into the room, happily chattering away.

'Hi, Humphrey! Gran said popcorn isn't good for hamsters, but I brought you this,' Phoebe said.

She slid a small piece of broccoli between the bars of my cage.

'THANKS-THANKS-THANKS!' I squeaked.

Now I knew for sure that Phoebe and Kelsey loved me!

The girls giggled and went back to talking about ancient Egypt.

'Let's make a club – just the two of us,' Kelsey suggested.

'With a secret name,' Phoebe said. 'And a secret handshake.'

It was pretty funny to watch them come up with a handshake. They crossed arms and hopped up and down.

They even tried doing it with their backs to each other.

Once, they got all twisted up like pretzels. Of course, they giggled hysterically.

Then they worked on a secret name. At first, they talked about taking the beginning letters of Kelsey's name and the last letters of Phoebe's name.

'The Kel-be Club?' Phoebe said. 'That doesn't sound like anything from *Secrets of the Nile.*'

Kelsey nodded. 'You're right. Hey, what about something to do with the Nile? The Nile Girls?'

Phoebe thought for a second. 'Sisters of the Nile?'

'Yay!' Kelsey clapped her hands in delight. 'Sisters of the Nile! I love it. Let's shake on it.'

Phoebe and Kelsey were very serious as they crossed their arms in front of themselves, shook both hands three times and bowed their heads.

So that was the secret handshake – and it wasn't a secret any more!

'That's good for meetings, but if people see us do the handshake, it won't be a secret any more,' Kelsey said. 'We need a secret signal for school,' she continued. 'Something no one will notice except us.'

They tried some pretty silly signals, but they finally decided on this: wave with the right hand, wiggle your fingers and wink.

I tried it and believe me, it's not easy, especially because I have to stop and think which is my right paw and which is my left. And I have four paws to keep track of.

Once I had that figured out, I tried to wiggle my fingers. Of course, I don't have fingers, so I had to wiggle my toes.

Hamsters don't usually wink (except for a hamster I know named Winky), but I tried it a few times and found I could do that, too.

I guess Phoebe saw me practising.

'I think Humphrey's trying the secret greeting,' she said. 'Maybe we should let him in the club.'

Kelsey giggled. 'Don't be silly. He doesn't know the secret *word* – remember?'

She whispered in her friend's ear and Phoebe nodded.

Then Kelsey added, 'Anyway, we're Sisters of the Nile and he's a boy. Besides that, he's a hamster!'

Suddenly, my whiskers wilted and I didn't feel so great.

I went back into my sleeping hut to think things over.

I stayed there a long time, but I didn't sleep.

The next day, Phoebe watched me spin on my wheel and let me roll around her room in my hamster ball.

Later, she and her grandmother sat in front of the computer and talked to Phoebe's mum.

'Kelsey and I dressed up like mummies! And we started a club called Sisters of the Nile. We even have a secret signal! I'll show you.' Phoebe waved her right hand, wiggled her fingers and winked.

Phoebe's mum laughed.

She wasn't actually in the house. She was FAR-FAR-FAR away in the army.

Phoebe's dad was in the army, too. Phoebe's mum said he'd call the next night.

'The club sounds fun. What else is new?' Phoebe's mum asked.

'Ooh, you'll never guess! *Humphrey*'s here

for the weekend!' Phoebe said.

Mum chuckled. 'The famous Humphrey that you talk about all the time?'

Even though she was FAR-FAR-FAR away, she'd heard of me!

Phoebe took me out of the cage and held me right up to the camera.

'Greetings!' I squeaked and Phoebe's mum laughed.

I could see her now. She wore a camouflage uniform and had a really big smile.

'He's one handsome hamster,' she said.

What an unsqueakably clever woman!

Phoebe put me back in the cage.

'He's a great hamster, but he's not in the club, because he's a boy and a hamster,' she explained.

Ouch! That still hurt. What's wrong with a girl who's a human being in a club with a boy who's a hamster?

Phoebe kept on talking for a while and then she said, 'I love you, Mum. Come home soon!'

After the call was over and we were alone, I heard Phoebe whisper, 'Please Mum and Dad. *Please come home soon.*'

Humphrey's Top Secret Scribbles

Secrets, secrets everywhere,
Make me think my friends don't care.

5

Secret Greetings, Secret Meetings

'Watch carefully, Og,' I told my froggy friend when Phoebe brought me back to Room 26 on Monday. 'You might see some strange things going on.'

'BOING!' Og replied, which I think meant he was going to watch.

It wasn't long before Mrs Brisbane opened the door to Room 26 and the students started coming in.

'Watch what Phoebe does when Kelsey comes in,' I squeaked to Og.

'BOING-BOING!' Og said.

'Hi, Humph!' Slow-Down-Simon said as he

raced past my cage, in a hurry as always.

When Just-Joey came in, he walked straight to my cage.

'Hi, Humphrey,' he said. 'Did you have a good weekend? Guess what – I saw a great TV show last night about elephants! Boy, do I want to see elephants in the wild someday.'

I've never seen an elephant but from what I've heard, they are MUCH-MUCH-MUCH bigger than dogs or even camels. I don't think I'd care to see one *anywhere* . . . especially not in the wild!

'BOING!' I don't think Og wanted to meet an elephant, either.

I looked at the door and saw Kelsey coming in. She headed for the cloakroom to take off her coat.

'Kelsey's here, Og. Be on the lookout for Phoebe,' I said.

Joey giggled when he heard our conversation. 'Of course, I like hamsters and frogs the best,' he said.

He's one unsqueakably clever boy!

Just then Og sounded the alarm. 'BOING-BOING-BOING-BOING!'

Kelsey was coming in the door.

'Thanks! Now – watch!' I told my neighbour.

As I expected, Phoebe raised her right hand. Kelsey raised hers, too.

Then they wiggled their fingers and winked. Next, they giggled, which wasn't part of the secret signal.

'BOING!' Og sounded surprised.

'What's this for?' Rolling-Rosie raised her fingers and wiggled them, too.

'Oh, it's nothing,' Phoebe answered. 'We were just waving.'

'It was more than that. Come on, tell me,' Rosie insisted.

'We can't,' Kelsey said. 'It's a secret. A secret club.'

'Can I be in it?' Rosie asked.

Kelsey and Phoebe didn't answer right away.

Finally, Kelsey said, 'If we let everybody in, it won't be a secret any more.'

When Kelsey and Phoebe turned away, I could see how upset Rosie was.

'BOING-BOING!' Og said.

I don't think he liked what he saw, either.

'Og, it's a signal they planned at Phoebe's

house,' I explained. I glanced at Og and I was positive that he wasn't smiling.

SPLASH! He dived into the water side of his tank and began to swim.

I wasn't smiling, either.

I hopped on my wheel and began to spin as fast as I could.

The next morning before class began, Stop-Talking-Sophie came over to my cage. She does love to talk.

'Hi, Humphrey! Did you have a good sleep last night? I'll bet it's boring in here when we're gone. I hope I get to take you home soon,' she said.

She talked so fast, I couldn't get a squeak in.

Then Rolling-Rosie joined her.

'Sophie, would you like to start a secret club?' she asked. 'Just you and me?'

Sophie's eyes lit up. 'Oh, yes! I'd love to!'

'Let's talk about it at lunchtime,' Rosie said.

As she rolled her wheelchair away, Sophie turned back to me. 'Did you hear that? Isn't that great?'

'GREAT-GREAT-GREAT!' I agreed.

Sophie leaned in close to my cage. 'I still miss my old school and my best friend there – Annie. I keep asking my parents if we can move back.'

I didn't know that Sophie was new to Longfellow School or that she missed her best friend.

'But if I have Rosie for a new best friend . . .' Sophie didn't finish because the bell rang and class began.

Mrs Brisbane began the day with our HARD-HARD-HARD vocabulary words.

At least now I knew that *papyrus* was like paper and that *hieroglyphics* was a way to write, using hieroglyphs.

And I knew that the *pyramids* were huge stone buildings and *pharaohs* were kings.

That didn't make those words any easier to spell, though.

Mrs Brisbane gave my friends sheets of paper where they had to fill in the blanks with the right words.

Then she said, 'Class, we're taking a little break from ancient Egypt. It's time to go to the library. If you have books to return, get them out now.'

My classmates took their library books and lined up.

Thomas had the most books. 'Look, Mrs Brisbane,' he said. 'I've finished all of these.'

'I want to check out a mummy book,' Simon said.

'Me too!' Hurry-Up-Harry said. 'And I'm going to get there first!'

Usually, Simon is three steps ahead of Harry, but this time Harry was right by his side.

Mrs Brisbane smiled, and soon, Og and I were alone in the classroom again.

As much as I like Og, I would have rather gone to the library with my friends. I'm too small to reach the tall shelves, but I like looking up at row after row of books.

Tall books, small books, short books, long books. Books with pictures. Books without pictures. I only wished I could pick one out for myself.

Every day, Mrs Brisbane read aloud to the class. That was my favourite time of day – especially when it was an unsqueakably exciting story!

·o·

When my friends came back, they were all clutching library books and chattering loudly.

'I got a mummy book!' Simon shouted as he rushed into the room.

'I got one, too!' Harry held up his book.

'So did I!' Nicole waved her book under Mrs Brisbane's nose. 'See, there are great pictures!'

Sometimes Not-Now-Nicole isn't very patient.

'I'll look at it later,' Mrs Brisbane told her.

I never knew there were so many books about mummies!

'I got a book all about what it was like to live in ancient Egypt,' Tall-Paul said.

'Humphrey, I got a book about a hamster,' Stop-Talking-Sophie said as she passed by my cage. 'Maybe I'll read it to you!'

'Please, do!' I squeaked and I meant it.

Everyone seemed so excited about their books . . . except for one.

Joey was the last to return to the classroom. He wasn't smiling or chattering but he did have a small, thin book in his hand.

'What book did you choose?' Mrs Brisbane asked him.

Joey wrinkled his nose and looked down at the book. 'Um, just a book.'

'What book?' I squeaked at the top of my lungs. Unfortunately, my voice isn't very loud.

'It's, um, a book about, um, a rabbit,' he said softly.

Mrs Brisbane leaned down and looked at the book. 'Oh, yes,' she said. '*The New Adventures of Robot the Rabbit*. Haven't you read this already?'

Joey stared down at his shoes. 'Maybe I have. It was pretty good.'

'It is good,' Mrs Brisbane said. 'But next time, try a new book. There are so many good ones in the library.'

Joey didn't look up. 'Okay,' he said.

Mrs Brisbane patted him on the shoulder and Joey hurried back to his table.

'A *robot* that is also a *rabbit*?' I squeaked.

I didn't mind Joey reading a book about a rabbit or a robot, but I minded him looking so unhappy. I guess Mrs Brisbane felt the same way.

When my classmates were rushing out of Room 26 for lunch, Mrs Brisbane stopped Joey.

'Can we talk alone for a minute?' she asked.

He nodded.

'Why don't you eat your lunch here?' she asked. 'Should I get you some milk?'

Joey shook his head. 'No, I have it in my lunchbox.'

Soon, Mrs Brisbane and Joey were sitting at his table, eating their sandwiches.

It was always funny to see Mrs Brisbane sitting in a student chair. She wasn't that tall for a human and in a student chair she looked, well . . . almost like a student!

'I have tuna,' Mrs Brisbane said after taking a bite of her sandwich. 'How about you?'

Joey swallowed a bite of his sandwich. 'Cheese,' he said.

'So, Joey, I wanted to ask you about your library books,' she said. 'The Robot the Rabbit books are good, but you've read them already. Why do you like to read them over and over?'

Joey took a bite out of his sandwich and spent a long time chewing it. 'Robot the

Rabbit's funny,' he finally said. 'And he has great adventures.'

Mrs Brisbane pushed a pile of yummy-looking carrot sticks toward Joey. 'Have some,' she said.

I wouldn't have minded having a carrot myself! I guess loving carrots is something I have in common with rabbits. Though probably not robots.

Joey took one and nibbled.

'Did Mr Fitch help you look for something new?' she asked.

Mr Fitch is the school librarian and he knows *everything* about books!

'Yes,' Joey said. 'He showed me a lot of books: a pirate book and a book about a football team and a book about landing on the moon.'

'Those sound good.' Mrs Brisbane crunched on her carrot.

Joey didn't say anything. They ate in silence for a minute.

'If you tried something new, you could still read Robot the Rabbit books once in a while,' Mrs Brisbane said.

Joey put his sandwich down. 'Maybe . . . I'm

getting a little too old for them.'

Mrs Brisbane nodded. 'I think you could try something at your reading level. What about a mummy book, like Simon and Harry and Nicole are reading?'

Joey shook his head. I guess he wasn't very interested in reading about mummies.

I have to say, I don't want to read book about mummies, either, because they sound unsqueakably scary!

Mrs Brisbane wiped her mouth with her napkin. 'Joey, I'd like you to challenge yourself with your reading. Will you try?'

Joey stared down at his desk, but he nodded his head. 'Yes,' he whispered.

'Great!' Mrs Brisbane said.

The bell rang and Mrs Brisbane stood up.

'I'm so glad we had this talk, aren't you?'

Joey nodded.

I think Just-Joey is a very honest person, but at that moment, I'm not sure he was telling the truth.

And then, he spoke up. 'Mrs Brisbane? Maybe I'm not very good at reading.'

Mrs Brisbane looked surprised. 'Really? Your

marks could be a little better, but they're not that bad.'

Joey shrugged again. 'I don't know,' he said. 'But when I read a book, I never seem to get anywhere.'

Mrs Brisbane looked at Joey for a while before she answered. 'We'll work on that,' she said. 'Together.'

Joey looked a little happier then.

But I have to squeak the truth: I felt BAD-BAD-BAD.

'You won't tell anybody, will you? About my not liking to read?' Joey asked.

'No, it will be our little secret,' Mrs Brisbane answered.

After school was over, I jiggled my lock-that-doesn't-lock and scrambled over to Og's tank.

'I can't imagine not liking to read,' I squeaked.

As soon as I said it, I realized something. *I* can read (because I'm an unsqueakably clever hamster) but Og probably can't. Not because he's not clever. It's because he's a frog – and books don't hold up well in water!

'I've got to find a book Joey likes,' I said.

'BOING-BOING!' Og agreed.

But I'd have to wait until later that night, after Aldo left.

As soon as Aldo came into the room, he said, 'Guys, I really want to tell somebody my big secret.'

'Tell us!' I squeaked. 'Please!'

'I promised Maria I wouldn't tell anybody yet,' he said. 'But I'm about to burst!'

'Don't burst!' I said. 'That sounds messy!'

In the end, though, Aldo didn't tell us his secret.

And Mrs Brisbane didn't tell me her secret about what student would be leaving.

Not knowing someone's secret can make you feel terrible.

I'd seen the look on Rosie's face when she saw Phoebe and Kelsey with their secret signal and heard about their club.

And yet, I had my own secret: a secret mission.

I had to find a book for Joey.

And it couldn't be about Robot the Rabbit.

Humphrey's Top Secret Scribbles

Sometimes you have to LOOK-LOOK-LOOK
To find the very perfect book.

Secret Books, Secret Looks

When I got to the library, I was tempted to look at the *Secrets of the Nile* video again, but I was there to find a book for Joey.

It wouldn't be easy. I wasn't even sure what kind of book he would like.

And even if I knew, how would I possibly find the right one in the rows and rows and rows of books in the library?

'Don't mind me,' I greeted the fish, who were swimming in the glowing tank. 'I'm here to get a book.'

I REALLY-REALLY-REALLY hoped that I would find the right book for Joey.

And I REALLY-REALLY-REALLY hoped it would be on the bottom shelf, because it would be unsqueakably hard – or even impossible – to get to the high shelves.

Even just looking at the books on the lowest shelves would take a long time, because the library is a big place.

And it's not easy to read the titles when you're a small hamster on the floor and the names of the books on the shelves are sideways. I have to squinch my neck to one side to read them.

As I scurried along, I noticed that books were grouped together by subject. All the art books were together. All the history books were together. And all the sports books were together.

Mr Fitch is a very clever man to think of that!

But then suddenly all the books were different and I couldn't make sense of the titles. They weren't alike at all.

When I saw a Robot the Rabbit title, I realized that these books weren't about real things, like the art books and the history books. These books were stories!

Fiction. That's what the big label above the shelves said.

But the names on the books, next to the titles, were all grouped together.

So there were the B names: Babcock, Bedarski, Benjamin, Bowman.

Further on, there were the K names: Kantor, Kelly, Kendricks.

Those must be the authors' names and they were in the order of the alphabet, so BE came ahead of BO. And KA came before KE.

Mr Fitch is even more clever than I thought. I'll bet he can find any book in the library.

But could I find the right book for Joey?

I spent a good part of the night roaming around the library, hoping I'd see something that Joey would like.

When I saw light coming through the library windows, I scurried back to Room 26.

'I'm back!' I squeaked as I slid under the door.

'BOING-BOING-BOING!' Og sounded excited.

I glanced up at the clock.

Mrs Brisbane would be arriving soon!

I raced across the floor as fast as my legs could carry me, hopped up to grab the bottom of the long blinds' cord, and began swinging and swinging until I was level with the table.

Then I let go and leaped to the tabletop.

'I didn't find a book for Joey,' I squeaked to Og as I hurried to my cage. 'But I learned something about the library. I'll tell you later.'

I closed the door behind me and dived under my bedding.

Just then, I heard Mrs Brisbane say, 'Good morning, Humphrey and Og.'

I squeaked weakly and promptly went to sleep.

I took a longer nap than usual and when I woke up, Room 26 was buzzing with activity.

My friends had split up into their groups and were working on their projects.

Tall-Paul, Felipe and Holly were using modelling clay to make something that looked like a boat that curved up at the ends. They were with the Traders.

Sophie, Nicole and Small-Paul were in the group lining up jars and bottles of different sizes that would be painted. Of course – they were the Artists.

I knew that Phoebe was a Scribe, so the squiggly things she was drawing along with Cassie, Thomas and Daniel must have been the figures for the alphabet.

The Builders were using blocks of different sizes to make pyramids, but they were having a hard time getting the right shape.

'Slow-Down-Simon,' Kelsey said. 'We need to start again because it's going to be too small.'

'Yeah. We want a BIG pyramid,' Rolling-Rosie reminded him.

'Okay,' Simon said.

Then, Rosie did a very odd thing. She looked over at Sophie and, when she caught her eye, she circled her hand around her face, touched her shoulders with both hands, and nodded. Sophie did the exact same thing. And then they both giggled!

I wasn't the only one who noticed.

'What are you doing?' Kelsey asked.

'Oh, it's just a secret sign for our club,' Rosie said.

Kelsey looked surprised.

I was surprised, too.

'What club?' Simon asked.

'I can't tell you because you're not in it,' Rosie said.

Simon shrugged.

'You're copying Phoebe and me,' Kelsey said. 'You don't even know what our club is about.'

'And you don't know what our club is about,' Rosie replied. 'There's Sophie and Cassie and me, so far.'

'Come *on*. We'll never get anywhere if we don't get this started,' Simon complained.

'BOING-BOING!' Og twanged.

'I know,' I squeaked back. 'Rosie was upset when Kelsey and Phoebe wouldn't let her in the club, so she made up her own. But none of them are acting very nice.'

I glanced around the room. The Artists seemed to be a lot happier than the Builders.

Just-Joey seemed to be the happiest of all.

'I'm going to make a lion, because that's my favourite animal,' he said.

'That's good,' Small-Paul said. 'The Egyptians decorated a lot of things with animals.'

'I'm really glad I'm an Artist then,' Joey said.

'Because I like animals a *lot*. I think they're more interesting than people.'

'Oh, no!' I squeaked loudly. 'Humans are incredibly interesting!'

'Well, I want to put flowers on my jar,' Sophie said.

'Flowers?' Small-Paul replied. 'I don't think the Egyptians did that.'

Suddenly, I heard a lot of laughing and looked over at the Scribes.

'I've got another one,' I heard Thomas say. 'What did the baby pyramid say to the other pyramid?'

'What?' Cassie asked.

'How's your mummy?'

Everyone laughed again, including me.

'How about this one? Why are mummies good at their jobs? Because they get wrapped up in their work!' Thomas said.

That got an even bigger laugh.

'Where did you learn all these mummy jokes?' Daniel asked.

'In a joke book. I love joke books,' Thomas said. 'I love all kinds of books.'

'So do I,' Daniel said. 'Can I look at yours?'

'Sure,' Thomas said. 'Hey, here's another one: What do you call a mummy who eats cookies in bed?'

'I know that one,' Daniel replied. 'A crummy mummy!'

Mrs Brisbane came over to remind them to work on their hieroglyphs.

When she turned away, I saw Phoebe look over at Kelsey. She waved her right hand, wiggled her fingers and winked.

'What was that, Phoebe?' Mrs Brisbane asked.

I guess she saw her out of the corner of her eye.

Phoebe swallowed hard. 'I was waving to Kelsey.'

'That's a funny way to wave,' Mrs Brisbane said, but she didn't say anything more.

She continued on to the Artists' group. 'You're making a lot of progress,' she said. 'I can already tell that's a lion you're making, Joey.'

'Do you like my flowers, Mrs Brisbane?' Sophie asked. 'I'm going to make them all different colours.'

'I do, Sophie,' Mrs Brisbane said. 'But I'm not sure if the ancient Egyptians actually put flowers on their jars. Joey, why don't you go and ask Mr Fitch if he has more books with pictures of ancient Egyptian jars? Or something to show what kind of animals they had in Egypt back then.'

Joey looked surprised. 'He'd have a book like that?'

'I think so,' Mrs Brisbane said. 'Just ask him.'

Joey actually looked happy as he headed out the door.

He looked even happier when he came back with a BIG-BIG-BIG book.

'Wait till you see,' he told the other Artists. 'Falcons and baboons and *jackals*!'

He pointed to pictures in the books while Sophie and Small-Paul leaned in around him.

I was glad there was at least one book Joey liked.

But I still wanted to find him a book with a story in it that he liked.

One that wasn't about Robot the Rabbit.

'We should have a meeting for our secret club,' Rosie told Sophie and Cassie when they came back from lunch. 'Here's the sign for when we want to have a meeting.'

Then Rosie tapped the top of her head three times.

Sophie and Cassie giggled and tapped their heads three times.

Tall-Paul was listening to them talking, and soon I heard him ask Small-Paul if he wanted to start a secret club.

'We could make up a code and a secret signal. We could even make it Egyptian,' Tall-Paul explained. 'Maybe Felipe could be in it, too.'

'Great idea! But we need a name,' Small-Paul said. 'How about The Flying Pharaohs?'

Tall-Paul nodded and the two boys huddled together, so I couldn't hear any more.

'What's going on?' Thomas asked as he headed towards his table.

Tall-Paul and Small-Paul looked at each other, then looked at Thomas.

'Nothing,' Tall-Paul said.

'Nothing,' Small-Paul said.

Luckily, just then Mrs Brisbane told everyone

to take a seat so she could give out the homework assignment.

I was unsqueakably surprised when I heard what it was.

The homework was a riddle, but this riddle wasn't about a mummy.

It was about the Sphinx.

I loved learning about the pyramids with their treasures inside. I thought the mummy jokes were funny. And I loved pictures of the graceful boats that sailed down the Nile.

But I didn't like to think about the Sphinx. Especially after the dream I'd had.

'Class, remember that there was a Sphinx in ancient Greece? The Sphinx was usually shown as a female in Greece and a male in Egypt. And the Greek Sphinx always had a riddle.'

Thomas raised his hand and Mrs Brisbane called on him.

'I remember that the Sphinx guarded the city and if a stranger came and couldn't answer the riddle, something really bad happened.'

'That's right,' Mrs Brisbane said. 'And your homework for tonight is to solve one. Here is what the Sphinx asked: What creature walks on four legs in the morning, two legs in the afternoon and three legs in the evening?'

Most of my classmates turned and looked at Thomas.

He just shrugged. 'That one wasn't in the books I read.'

Mrs Brisbane wrote the riddle on the board and my friends copied it down.

I'm usually sad to see the other students leave at the end of the day, but that day, I was almost glad when the classroom was empty.

I didn't want to see any more of my friends whispering.

I didn't want to see any more of my other friends feeling left out.

And I wanted to work on the riddle.

Mrs Brisbane had already left, so I reached up behind my mirror for my notebook.

Suddenly, the door to the room opened, which surprised me, because it was way too early for Aldo to come in and clean.

I scrambled to the front of my cage and saw Ms Mac coming towards me.

Ms Mac is the wonderful human who brought me to Room 26 in the first place.

She was the one who told me that the students would learn a lot from me. She even told me I was handsome and clever.

I didn't know she was a supply teacher, so when she left, my heart was broken.

She was away a LONG-LONG-LONG time. But then she came back to teach first grade at Longfellow School and my heart feels a lot better now.

I love all my friends and Mrs Brisbane, too. But no one understands me like Ms Mac.

'Hey, Humphrey.' She smiled as she leaned in close to the cage. 'How's my buddy?'

There she was, with her bouncy black curls and her big dark eyes. She still smelled like apples.

I love apples and I love Ms Mac.

'HI-HI-HI!' I greeted her.

Og bounced up and down. 'BOING-BOING!'

'Oh, Og, I didn't mean to forget you. How's my favourite frog?' she asked.

It was fine with me if Og happened to be

Ms Mac's favourite frog. If she'd said he was her favourite animal, though, I might have felt a little bit jealous.

Ms Mac turned back to me. 'Humphrey, I have a secret to tell you. I love teaching first grade now, but I miss you!'

My whiskers quivered a little. 'I miss you, too, Ms Mac,' I squeaked.

'I thought of getting another hamster, but to tell you the truth, I don't think there's a hamster in the world that can measure up to you,' she said.

My tail wiggle-waggled.

'But I think the students in Room Twelve deserve a classroom pet. It would help them.' Ms Mac sighed. 'Maybe I'll get something different, like a turtle.'

Turtles are nice but they are extremely slow. It would take a long time for a turtle to teach students anything!

'Anyway, I've been thinking about you a lot, so I stopped by to say "Hi" and tell you I miss you,' she said. 'I'll come and see you again soon.'

'YES-YES-YES, please do!' I told her.

She started to leave, but then turned back.

'You know I wouldn't forget this,' she said as she reached into her coat pocket.

She opened the door to my cage and left a generous piece of apple on my bedding.

'Enjoy,' she said.

I couldn't wait to sink my teeth into its crunchy sweetness.

'I will,' I squeaked.

Ms Mac smiled. 'Oh, and please don't tell anybody what I said. It's just our little secret.'

Humphrey's Top Secret Scribbles

The Sphinx and her riddle give me quite a fright,
To solve her ancient secret, I might stay up all night!

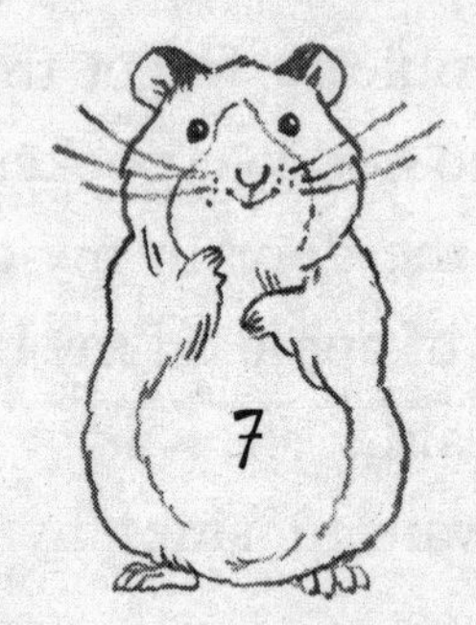

7

Secret Pages

'Og, you heard her secret, too,' I squeaked to my neighbour once we were alone.

Og splashed loudly.

'She said no other hamster can measure up to me,' I said.

'BOING-BOING!'

I was pretty sure Og agreed with her.

'But she still *might* get a class hamster.' I swallowed hard. 'I'm sorry to say that bothers me.'

'BOING-BOING-BOING!' Og sounded bothered, too.

'Of course, she might get a frog,' I continued.

Og suddenly leaped so high out of the water part of his tank, he almost popped its top.

'BOING!!!!'

I guess he didn't like the idea of Ms Mac getting a frog, either.

'There are so many secrets going on, my head is spinning like a hamster wheel,' I complained. 'And then there's that Riddle of the Sphinx! How on earth could the same creature walk on four legs in the morning, two legs in the afternoon and three legs in the evening?'

Really, it was perfectly ridiculous! Who ever heard of any creature walking on three legs?

'If you think of the answer, let me know!' I squeaked to Og.

Of course, even if he knew the answer, all I would hear would be BOING-BOING-BOING!

I was glad that Aldo worked quickly that night, because I needed time to answer the Riddle of the Sphinx for my homework. I also needed to find a book that Joey would love.

I hoped I could solve both of those problems in the same place: the library!

'Here I go, Og,' I squeaked as I slid under the door. 'Wish me luck!'

Even in the hallway, I could hear his loud 'BOING-BOING!'

It didn't take me long to scurry down the hallways of Longfellow School to reach the library.

'Hi! It's me – Humphrey,' I announced to the fish when I arrived in the library.

They floated around in their glowing tank as if they didn't notice me, so I went straight to work.

First, I needed to find out what kind of creature walked on four legs in the morning, two legs in the afternoon and three legs in the evening.

There are plenty of four-legged creatures, from elephants to hamsters!

And there are some two-legged animals, such as humans.

But I've never seen a three-legged animal or even a picture of one.

Even if I couldn't pull the big heavy books off the shelves, I might get an idea from the titles.

I scurried over to where I'd seen rows of animal books on my last visit. There they were: elephants and tigers and hippopotamuseses.

(I know I haven't got that right but I've tried.)

They all had the number 590 on them.

Those animals walk on four legs in the morning but I couldn't picture them on two legs in the afternoon!

There were books about birds. They walk on two legs in the afternoon, but they don't *have* four legs ever!

And then there were scary creatures, such as snakes, that don't have legs at all!

Come to think of it, neither did my fish friends in the library.

But none of them – from aardvarks to foxes to leopards to squirrels to zebras – walked on three legs!

I was puzzled because I didn't see hamsters and frogs in that section, but I found them later in the 636 section. No animals there had three legs, either.

I wasn't even getting close to answering the Riddle of the Sphinx, but I never realized there were so many interesting animals in the world! Hyenas, ocelots and prairie dogs! (I'm not too fond of dogs, though these looked more like hamsters.)

Then I had an idea about my other quest. 'Joey likes rabbits. And he loves his dog. Oh, and he likes Og and me, too!' I squeaked out loud. 'I think he'd like to read about animals. He was so happy to get the book about creatures in ancient Egypt.'

That could be it!

The fish opened and closed their mouths, but I didn't hear a thing.

Were they trying to tell me something? Maybe they could help me find an animal book for Joey. They ought to know the library pretty well. After all, they are library fish.

I scampered over, closer to their tank. 'Can you hear me?' I squeaked at the top of my tiny lungs.

They did have a glass wall and with all that water around them – maybe they couldn't hear me.

'The thing is, I need to find an animal story that Joey will like,' I shouted. 'He REALLY-REALLY-REALLY likes animals! I'm sure he likes fish, too!'

Their mouths opened and closed, but nothing came out that I could hear.

The tank was on a shelf behind the big desk where people check out books.

If I could only get a little closer to the tank, maybe the fish could hear me. But the desk was much taller than a regular desk. How could one small hamster get to the top?

I hurried around the back of the desk, where the librarian sat to check out books. There was a tall stool with long legs, but there was no way I could pull myself up to the top.

Then I noticed that there were many, many drawers on this side of the desk. And Mr Fitch had left some of them open. In fact, he had left most of them open.

Maybe he'd been in a hurry.

I started to come up with a Plan. And maybe, just maybe, my Plan would work.

I reached up with my front paws stretched towards the handle of the drawer closest to the floor and took hold.

Got it! I managed to swing one of my back paws up on the handle. Then I reached one of my front paws up to the edge of the drawer, made sure I had a firm grip and pulled myself up. Now I was standing with my back paws on the handle and my front paws on the edge of the drawer.

I swung my rear end back and forth until I was even with the top of the drawer and let go. Made it! I landed on a tall stack of notepads.

Standing on my tippy-toes, I grabbed the handle of the next drawer up.

I pulled myself up and vaulted over the top of the drawer and landed – plop – right in a box of tissues! That was a lucky break.

I rested for a few seconds, then used the tissues like a bouncy trampoline and bounced high enough for me to grab hold of the handle of the next drawer up.

Made it! This drawer had a stack of tins marked 'Stamp Pad' and a set of rubber stamps labelled, 'Donated by', 'Do Not Remove from Library' and 'Reference Only'.

They were unsqueakably interesting but I was only halfway up the desk, so I reached UP-UP-UP and pulled myself to the next drawer. This one had stacks of little notes printed with 'Hold For' and 'Book Overdue'.

Forgetful-Phoebe and Hurry-Up-Harry had

received a few of those Overdue notes, because they never managed to return their books on time.

Unfortunately, when I reached the next drawer, I fell into a jumble of things: paperclips and staples, a bottle of glue, drawing pins – ouch – glad I didn't step on them! There were big clips and small clips, a box of labels, some batteries and a wrinkled piece of paper that turned out to be Fire Drill Instructions.

The books in Mr Fitch's library are very organized, but I think he needs to organize his drawers a bit!

I was almost at the top, so I took a deep breath, and grabbed on to the edge of the desk. Then I PULLED-PULLED-PULLED myself up and there I was, sitting on top of the tall desk along with stacks of books, a telephone, a computer and several pencils.

Right behind me was the fish tank, glowing so brightly the light hurt my eyes.

I rested for a few seconds, chewing on a bit of celery I had tucked away in my cheek pouch.

When I felt stronger, I scurried closer to the

fish tank and looked up.

My, the fish were very beautiful. They were blue, pink, orange and yellow. There were striped fish and fish with polka dots.

I stared and stared as they circled around the tank, opening and closing their mouths.

I remembered my Plan and so I began to shout. 'Fish friends, I am a classroom hamster. One of my classmates, Joey, doesn't think he likes books. I think he would love an animal story from the fiction section. You live in the library. Do you have any ideas?'

They kept on circling and opening and closing their mouths.

One of them, with a bright blue body and white stripes, caught my eye.

'Did you hear me?' I shouted.

If I kept it up, I'd probably lose my voice.

Still looking at me, he opened and closed his mouth.

It looked as if he was talking but I couldn't hear anything but the BUBBLE-BUBBLE-BUBBLE sound the tank made.

I sighed. I was disappointed to learn that the fish weren't going to be helpful at all.

I'd worked very hard to get up to the top of the desk and my Plan had failed.

So I sat for a while, trying to figure out what to do next.

I didn't want to see the fish opening and closing their mouths but saying nothing, so I turned away.

That's when I started to notice the books that were stacked on the checkout desk.

Some of them had wonderful titles, such as *If You Lived on the Moon*, and *The Mysterious Magic Wand*. I'm not sure if I'd like to live on the moon, but I'd like to read about it. And if I had a magic wand, helping my friends would be a lot easier!

I walked around to see the other books on the desk.

A book about a girl with funny red plaits that curled up at the ends.

A book about rocks.

But the next book I saw got my attention.

There was a little boy on the dark red cover. He had big eyes, just like Joey's.

And he was surrounded by animals: a bear, a snake, a panther and a tiger!

The Jungle Book was the title and it was written by someone with a very strange name (at least to me). It was Rudyard Kipling.

A boy who lives in the jungle and is friends with the animals? All kinds of animals?

That sounded like a book Joey would like.

But how could a small hamster like me get a great big book to Room 26?

I sighed. My Plan had a giant glitch, because I'm so tiny. Joey might never get this book that was perfect for him!

Then, I remembered my trip up the drawers.

I'd seen rubber stamps and paperclips and sharp drawing pins.

And I'd also seen those notes that said 'Hold For'.

It wasn't easy, but I managed to hop my way back down one drawer.

There they were! 'Hold For' notes.

I carefully pulled one off the top, held it in my teeth, and pulled myself up to the next drawer and back to the desktop.

I set the 'Hold For' note on the desk and I grabbed a pencil.

I'm used to writing with the tiny pencil that

goes with my notebook. This was a BIG-BIG-BIG pencil, but I could lift it with two paws.

It took a long time, but I managed to write Joey's name.

My writing was small and shaky, but I was pleased when I looked at the note and saw:

HOLD FOR:
Joey
Rm. 26

I crossed my toes hard.

'Wish me luck!' I squeaked to the fish.

They didn't answer, but maybe they glowed a little more brightly.

Then I started my slow climb down the drawers, across the library floor and under the door, back to Room 26.

Back to the place I love best of all!

I was too tired when I got back to tell Og everything that had happened.

'Cross your fingers, um, paws, um, webbed feet that my Plan will work,' I said.

Og splashed around as I hurried back to the safety of my cage.

A little nap would have been nice, but I had too much on my mind. I pulled my notebook out from behind my little mirror.

I hadn't solved the Riddle of the Sphinx.

I wasn't sure if Joey would ever get *The Jungle Book*.

But I'd done my best and I had other things on my mind.

I opened my little notebook and began to write.

Human Secrets I Know About

- A student is leaving Room 26 soon. I don't know which student and I don't know when.

Question: Why is Mrs Brisbane happy about that? Because I am NOT-NOT-NOT!

- Aldo has a secret that his wife, Maria, told him. What is it? (No clue.)

- Joey's secret is that he doesn't enjoy reading. Will my Plan work?

- Secret Clubs: They started with Kelsey and Phoebe. Now Rosie, Cassie and Sophie have a secret club. So do Tall-Paul and Small-Paul. Feelings are being hurt. How to stop that?

- Ms Mac has a secret longing to have a class pet. Will she get another hamster? Will she love it more than she loves me?

My Secrets

- I write my secret thoughts in this wonderful little notebook. But I don't let anyone else see it.

- I have a lock-that-doesn't-lock and I hope no one ever discovers that secret, either.

Question: Are secrets good? Or are they bad?

Humphrey's Top Secret Scribbles

Secrets, secrets everywhere,
Should they stay secret, or should I share?

8

Secrets, Secrets Everywhere

'So who's solved the Riddle of the Sphinx?' Mrs Brisbane asked the next morning.

I certainly didn't raise my paw, but I was surprised to see almost every hand go up.

I was amazed. Were there actually any three-legged creatures?

'I wonder how many of you figured it out on your own and how many looked it up,' the teacher said. 'How about you, Thomas?'

'I looked it up, but I already knew it. I read it in a book,' Thomas said.

'Paul F., did you look it up?' Mrs Brisbane asked.

Paul looked down at the desk. He seemed embarrassed.

'I didn't say you couldn't look it up,' Mrs Brisbane said. 'In fact, if you couldn't solve it on your own, I think it would be clever to look it up.'

Small-Paul and most of the students in the class looked relieved.

'I would have looked it up in the library, but I couldn't find the right book,' I squeaked.

Mrs Brisbane looked over at my cage and smiled. 'I wonder if Humphrey knows the answer,' she said.

'No, but I wish I did!' I replied.

Of course, all she heard was SQUEAK-SQUEAK-SQUEAK.

'So who is going to tell me: What creature walks on four legs in the morning, two legs in the afternoon and three legs in the evening?' Mrs Brisbane asked.

Hands were waving everywhere, but she called on Stop-Talking-Sophie.

'I looked it up online and the answer is Humans, because the beginning of life is like the morning, when people are babies and they crawl on all fours. In the afternoon, when they're older, they walk on two legs. And in the evening, when they're very old, people sometimes walk with a cane. Once you know the answer it seems easy. But before I looked it up, it seemed impossible to answer at all,' Sophie answered without even taking a breath.

'That's true, Sophie,' Mrs Brisbane said. 'I think all riddles seem easy once you know the answer. But the legend is that many travellers lost their lives because they couldn't figure it out.'

Rosie raised her hand. 'Why didn't the travellers look it up?'

'They couldn't go online back then,' Thomas said. 'They didn't have computers that long ago. I read about it in a book, but they probably didn't have books, either.'

'They didn't have books the way we do,' our teacher explained. 'They had papyrus. It was very expensive, so hardly anyone had any. Students who were learning to write practised on bits of stone.'

Thomas groaned. 'That would really make your backpack heavy!'

That made everyone laugh, including Mrs Brisbane.

I was glad I had my little notebook, which hardly weighed a thing. Imagine if a small hamster had to write on stones!

Next, Mrs Brisbane taught maths, but it was a very funny kind of maths they used in ancient Egypt. Instead of numbers, they used symbols and there were only seven of them.

Each 1 was a single line. That was easy, but as the numbers moved up, the symbols were stranger and stranger. A coil of rope stood for a 10.

A finger represented 10,000, which is a very large number.

When Mrs Brisbane showed us the symbol for 100,000, Og let out an extra-loud 'BOING!'

The symbol for 100,000 was a frog!

'BOING-BOING-BOING!'

Of course, my friends all laughed.

When Mrs Brisbane finished showing us all of the symbols, I was disappointed that one of them was not a hamster.

But I was happy there was at least a frog. Really.

Mrs Brisbane put up some maths problems for the class to solve using the symbols.

Near the end of the class, Mr Fitch appeared, carrying a book.

I scrambled up to the tippy top of my cage and saw that the book had a dark red cover. I crossed my toes and hoped.

'Sorry to interrupt,' he said. 'I found this book with a hold slip for Joey in Room Twenty-six. I thought I'd bring it down in case he needs it.'

First Just-Joey looked surprised. Then he frowned and shook his head. 'Not for me.'

Mr Fitch walked to Joey's table and handed him the book. 'It's a good one,' he said.

Joey took the book.

The slip I'd written on was still tucked inside and Joey read it.

'Thanks,' he said, but he looked confused.

'Thanks!' I squeaked.

'What's the book?' Mrs Brisbane asked when Mr Fitch was gone.

'It's called *The Jungle Book*,' Joey said. 'It has a lot of animals in it.'

Mrs Brisbane looked pleased.

And I was HAPPY-HAPPY-HAPPY that my Plan had worked.

But I still wasn't sure that Joey would like the book.

Mrs Brisbane kept on talking but Joey wasn't listening.

He opened the book and stared at the first page.

I think that Mrs Brisbane knew that Joey wasn't listening, but she didn't say anything.

Joey turned the page.

I crossed my toes again.

My poor toes were aching by the time Mrs Brisbane split the class up into their groups.

I wanted to keep track of Joey and the book, but there were so many things going on, I forgot.

First Phoebe waved her hand at Kelsey, wiggled her fingers and winked. I guess Kelsey forgot that she was helping to hold up the blocks for the pyramid. She started to return the signal while Simon was gluing the next one on.

The pyramid collapsed into a heap of blocks.

'Now look what you've done!' Simon said.

I didn't blame him for being irritated. Rosie was annoyed as well.

'What happened?' Mrs Brisbane asked when she rushed over to their table.

'Kelsey let go,' Simon said.

'It was an accident,' Kelsey said.

'Well, Be-Careful-Kelsey,' Mrs Brisbane said. 'Help Simon and Rosie set it up again.'

The room was peaceful for a few minutes, but then Joey shouted, 'Hey, watch out, Sophie! You almost got paint on my book.'

When I glanced at Sophie, she was looking at Rosie. Both of them had very red faces.

Mrs Brisbane hurried over to the Artists. 'What's happened here?'

'She's acting strange,' Joey said. 'She was making these weird moves. I think she flipped out or something.'

'Joey! That's not a nice thing to say,' Mrs Brisbane said.

'I think there was a fly buzzing around my head or maybe it was a bee or a mosquito, and I was trying to wave it away and I spilled some paint but not on his book,' Sophie explained.

I think that she was performing her secret

sign for her secret club.

Once the class was back at work and Mrs Brisbane was talking to the Scribes, Small-Paul, Tall-Paul and Fix-It-Felipe spread their arms like wings and said something that sounded really strange. I think I heard 'Flying Pharaohs' in the middle.

That made Joey look up from his book and frown. Maybe it was because they interrupted his reading, but maybe he wants to be in a secret club, too.

Holly watched all the strange signals, too, and she didn't look happy about it, either.

Just before the bell rang, while my friends were cleaning up their tables, Thomas tapped Joey on the shoulder and pointed at the book.

'I read that one,' he said. 'Do you like it?'

'It's pretty cool. I'd like to live in the jungle with those animals,' Joey said. 'But it's awfully long.'

Thomas shrugged. 'So what? It doesn't matter how long a book is. You start at the beginning and keep reading until you get to the end. When you get to the end, you start another book.'

Joey thought for a moment and then he grinned. 'I can do that.'

It had been an unsqueakably strange day but at least one thing had turned out right.

Joey liked a book!

When the room was empty, I hopped on my wheel and spun as fast as I could.

I was going so fast, at first I didn't notice that Mr Morales had come into Room 26.

He was talking to Mrs Brisbane near the door.

Sometimes I wish I had a brake on my hamster wheel, but I spun slower and slower until I could hop off and listen.

'So far, it looks as if the plan will work out,' Mr Morales said. 'I got this from her mum today.'

He handed Mrs Brisbane a piece of paper.

'Wonderful,' she said as she read it. 'Oh, the whole class will love this!'

'We might even get the local television station to cover it,' he said. 'There's never been anything like this at Longfellow School.

But the important thing is, *we have to keep it a secret.*'

Mrs Brisbane put a finger on her lips. 'My lips are sealed,' she said.

That couldn't be true, because if her lips were sealed, she couldn't talk! Humans say the strangest things sometimes.

'You hear that, Humphrey and Og?' Mr Morales pointed towards our table. 'Not a peep out of you about the secret!'

I like Mr Morales and he is the Most Important Person at Longfellow School, but I had to squeak up for myself.

'I don't even know the secret!' I squeaked at the top of my small lungs. 'And I don't say "peep" and neither does Og!'

'BOING-BOING,' my froggy friend agreed.

Mr Morales chuckled. 'I guess he's saying the secret is safe with him.'

Well, he was WRONG-WRONG-WRONG about that!

After more talking, they both left Room 26 for the day.

Og and I were alone at last.

I jiggled my lock-that-doesn't-lock and

scampered over to Og's tank. 'I don't understand,' I squeaked. 'Why is everyone so happy that one of our students is leaving?'

Og splashed and splashed and I had to scurry away to keep from getting wet. I don't ever want to get wet!

When he settled down, I moved closer again.

'But did you hear what Mr Morales said? He said *her* mum. So the person leaving is a girl!'

'BOING-BOING-BOING!' Og boomed.

I didn't want one of the girls to leave our class, either. I didn't want anyone to leave.

'And why would the television station come, just because one girl is leaving?' I continued. 'I thought reporters usually cover car chases and weather and a market where you can buy socks. Although why they report on the Sock Market every day seems weird to me.'

'BOING!' Og agreed.

I realized that Aldo would be coming to clean soon, so I hurried back to my cage and slammed the door behind me.

Before long, I heard the RATTLE-RATTLE-RATTLE of his cleaning trolley.

The door opened and when he switched on

the lights, the room was as bright as it was during the day.

'Hey, how are my favourite students in Room Twenty-six?' he asked.

Before I could answer, he was busily sweeping the floor. I watched Aldo carefully as he worked because I knew he had a secret, too. And maybe he would give us a clue like Mrs Brisbane did.

But his lips were sealed. He didn't say a word – or a peep!

When he was gone, I opened my little notebook and, by the glow of the streetlights, I added some things to my list.

Human Secrets I Know About

- A student is leaving Room 26 soon. I don't know which student and I don't know when.

It's a girl.

Sophie still misses her old school. What if she's going back?

Kelsey's dad wants to take the whole

family to New York City. Maybe they're moving there?

Question: Why would they send a television reporter to cover either of those?

I nibbled on my pencil for a minute. Then I added something that made me happy.

- Joey's secret is that he doesn't enjoy reading. Will my Plan work?

YES, I think it will.

Humphrey's Top Secret Scribbles

A girl will be leaving us any day,
Is there some way to make her stay?

9 Secret Games and Scary Ghosts

For the rest of the week, Room 26 seemed out of control.

The groups made progress on their projects. The Traders' boat began to look a little bit like a real boat. The paintings on the Artists' jars started to look like animals. The Builders' pyramid only collapsed two more times. But the Scribes argued a *lot* about their hieroglyphs.

'We need a frog,' Phoebe insisted.

'BOING-BOING!' Og agreed.

'If we have a frog, we need a hamster,' Thomas said.

Daniel disagreed. 'A hamster is too hard to draw.'

'You need to TRY-TRY-TRY!' I told them.

No one was listening.

And Mrs Brisbane, who was always in control of our class, was a little bit confused.

'Phoebe? Are you raising your hand?' she asked as Phoebe and Kelsey exchanged secret signals.

'Rosie? Do you need some help?' she asked when Sophie touched her shoulders to signal to Rosie.

And when Felipe and Small-Paul spread their arms out like wings, Mrs Brisbane said, 'Boys, be careful!'

'Mrs Brisbane, those are secret signals for secret clubs!' I insisted.

Of course, she couldn't understand me.

Then there were those other secrets.

Ms Mac came to visit again one afternoon. She didn't have much to say. She sat next to the table and stared at me.

'What do you want?' I asked her. 'If you

don't mind my saying so, it's not polite to stare.'

Ms Mac sighed. 'Oh, Humphrey, I'm having so much trouble deciding on a classroom pet for Room Twelve.'

'Let me help,' I said.

But of course, she had no idea what I was squeaking.

And there was Aldo.

He came in to clean every night and he did a GREAT-GREAT-GREAT job. But he also complained about his secret.

'*Mamma mia*,' he said one night. 'This good news is hard to keep secret, but a promise is a promise.'

'You know I won't tell anyone,' I said. Which was true, because humans can't understand me, anyway. 'And neither will Og.'

'BOING-BOING-BOING!' my neighbour agreed.

But Aldo didn't share his secret.

It's a very good thing to be able to keep a secret. But it's a very bad thing to know that someone has a secret that he won't share.

I was glad when Friday finally arrived, and I

think Mrs Brisbane was happy as well.

'Who is taking Humphrey home?' she asked.

Tall-Paul waved his hand. He looked unsqueakably happy.

'Sorry to leave you here alone,' I squeaked to Og as Tall-Paul carried me out of Room 26.

I heard a distant 'BOING-BOING!' as the door closed behind us.

Tall-Paul is by far the tallest student in Room 26.

He's almost as tall as Mrs Brisbane. In fact, he's almost as tall as Mr Morales!

So I was unsqueakably surprised when I got to his house and discovered that compared with the rest of the Green family, he wasn't tall at all. In fact, he looked short!

This was one tall family! It was like being surrounded by giants – at least to a short hamster like me.

But they were very *friendly* giants. And I was HAPPY-HAPPY-HAPPY that they didn't have any gigantic pets.

In the evening, Tall-Paul and his tall parents

sat by my cage, so I put on a show for them.

First, I spun on my wheel. Then, I hopped off and climbed up the side of my cage to the top. Next, I climbed down my tree branch, back to the wheel, and started spinning again.

'Watching Humphrey is much better than watching TV,' Mrs Green said.

Mr Green agreed. 'It's like watching a one-hamster circus.'

They were friendly and *clever* giants.

'I told you he was fun,' Paul said. 'So can I get a hamster now?'

'Let's see how the weekend goes,' his father answered.

I thought it would be wonderful if Paul got a hamster. I decided I'd do everything I could to prove that hamsters make pawsitively wonderful pets!

The next day, Paul's mum asked if he wanted to invite some friends over.

'Paul Fletcher,' Tall-Paul quickly answered. 'And Felipe.'

'I'll call them,' Mrs Green said. 'And any

one else? How about Thomas?'

Tall-Paul thought for a few seconds and then shook his head. 'No, just Paul F. and Felipe.'

'I thought you were friends with Thomas, too,' his mum said. 'And Joey.'

'I am.' Paul hesitated. 'But this time I just want Paul and Felipe to come over.'

Mrs Green looked puzzled but she didn't say anything more.

She left and came back a few minutes later to say that Paul F.'s mother would bring both boys to the house.

When Small-Paul and Felipe arrived, they came into the bedroom and Tall-Paul closed the door.

'My mum wanted me to invite Thomas and Joey, too,' Tall-Paul said. 'But I talked her out of it. If they came, we couldn't do our secret club things.'

'Oh, I almost forgot,' Small-Paul said. He spread his arms like wings and so did Tall-Paul and Felipe.

'*Bata-wata-fata*!' they all chanted.

I don't think it was really Egyptian. I think it

was something they made up.

'Flying Pharaohs for ever!' they added, and they bowed to each other.

Then they acted normal again.

'So this is our first real meeting,' Tall-Paul said. 'What do you want to do?'

Felipe shrugged. 'I don't know. Something pharaohs would do, I guess.'

'I have an idea,' Tall-Paul said. 'I was reading about ancient Egypt and they played one of the earliest board games.'

'Cool,' Small-Paul said. 'What did it look like?'

Soon the friends were on Paul Green's computer.

'There it is,' Tall-Paul said. 'It's called Senet. They even found games in some pharaohs' tombs.'

'I bet I could make one of those,' Fix-It-Felipe said.

There wasn't much he couldn't build. 'Let *me* see!' I squeaked.

The boys laughed but I was feeling very frustrated because I couldn't see the computer screen from my cage.

'Wow, look at the one they found in King Tut's tomb!' Tall-Paul exclaimed. 'It's beautiful.'

Felipe began to sketch. 'We'll need a big cardboard box. And game pieces,' he said.

Tall-Paul found a box while Small-Paul got out some other board games and borrowed the game pieces from them.

'And little sticks to throw,' Small-Paul said.

'How about pencils? Or big paperclips?' Tall-Paul suggested.

'Paperclips would work for now,' Felipe agreed.

The boys also gathered a ruler and markers as Felipe began to make the game board.

'The path around it looks something like a snake,' Small-Paul said.

'Eeek!' I squeaked. It slipped out when I heard the word 'snake'.

I relaxed when I realized he wasn't talking about a real snake.

The three friends spent the afternoon making the game and then playing it.

I dozed off for a while, but woke up once when I heard Paul F. shout, 'Take that, Tutankhamen!'

I fell back to sleep until Paul G. shouted, 'Bad move, Amenhotep!'

I guessed that Amenhotep was another pharaoh.

'Hey, what about Humphrey?' Felipe asked. 'I'll bet he wants to play.'

He gently took me out of my cage and set me on the game board. It looked a little bit like an obstacle course.

I wasn't sure what I was supposed to do, but I saw the game pieces on different squares.

Aha! The goal of the game must be to knock each of them over.

So I scurried from square to square and knocked them down, one by one.

Every time a game piece fell, the boys laughed.

'You win, Humphrey,' Tall-Paul said when all the pieces had fallen. 'Even the pharaohs never played a game like that.'

'Gee, I'd love to show the game to Mrs Brisbane,' Felipe said as he put me back in the cage. 'Maybe we'd get extra credit.'

Tall-Paul didn't agree. 'No! This is a Flying Pharaohs game. We have to keep it a secret.'

'Right,' Small-Paul said. 'Everything that happens in the Flying Pharaohs Club is a secret.'

When Small-Paul's mum came to pick the boys up, Tall-Paul put the board in a drawer.

'Don't you tell anyone our secret, Humphrey,' he told me. 'Or the ghost of King Tut will come after you.'

My whiskers wiggled and my tail twitched. 'Eeek!' I squeaked.

'Oh, Humphrey, I was joking,' Tall-Paul said.

It wasn't a very funny joke – at least to a small creature like me.

I scrambled under my bedding and I stayed there a LONG-LONG-LONG time.

The next day was more fun.

Tall-Paul showed his parents how much he wanted a hamster by cleaning out my cage and giving me fresh food and water.

He took very good care of me and Mrs Green was impressed.

Then Tall-Paul and his dad made an obstacle course on the living room floor, using blocks and books to create barriers.

I ran that obstacle course over and over to show Paul's dad how much fun a hamster can be.

Even Paul's big sister and his BIG-BIG-BIG brother came in to watch.

Mr Green was impressed, and he gave me a lovely slice of apple once I was back in my cage.

'So can I have a hamster?' Paul asked his mum and dad before bedtime.

'Maybe,' they said.

'Maybe' isn't a very good answer. But they were smiling when they said it.

After Tall-Paul went to bed that night, I thought about all the things I had to tell my friend Og when I got back to Room 26.

But later, when the room was dark and the house was quiet, I thought I saw the ghost of King Tut in front of my cage.

I was too scared to squeak.

I raced into my sleeping hut and I didn't come out until the next morning.

Humphrey's Top Secret Scribbles

Kings and their treasures are quite nice
BUT . . .
I don't want to meet the ghost of King
Tut!

Whispered Secrets

'BOING-BOING-BOING!' Og greeted me when I returned to Room 26 on Monday morning.

'Yes, Og. I had a very nice time,' I replied. 'Sorry, I can't tell you everything, though, because part of it is a secret.'

Og suddenly leaped into the water side of his tank and splashed loudly.

'Goodness, Og, what's going on?' Mrs Brisbane asked as she came over to check on his tank.

Og quietened down a little.

Of course, I knew why he was splashing. He didn't like that I was keeping a secret from him.

Up until then, Og knew all my secrets – even the one about my lock-that-doesn't-lock.

He was feeling left out and I was feeling VERY-VERY-VERY guilty.

When my classmates were at playtime and Mrs Brisbane left the room for a moment, I had to talk to him.

'Og, I'll tell you the secret. On Saturday, Small-Paul and Felipe came over for their secret club and they made a board game from ancient Egypt and I played, too. But Tall-Paul said if I told anybody, King Tut's ghost would come after me,' I squeaked.

Og let out a huge 'BOING!'

'But I'm not scared of a silly old ghost,' I said. I crossed my toes because what I was saying wasn't true. Just because I'd never seen a ghost didn't mean there couldn't be one.

'BOING-BOING-BOING!' Og sounded worried.

'And I'm not keeping secrets from you ever again,' I told him.

'BOING-BOING!'

'You're welcome,' I replied.

A very happy-looking Mrs Brisbane came back to Room 26, carrying some papers.

'Get ready for some excitement, boys,' she said.

I knew she was talking to Og and me, because we were the only boys there.

'WHAT-WHAT-WHAT?' I asked.

'You'll see,' she said.

Then, Mrs Wright, the PE teacher, walked in.

Mrs Wright isn't a bad human, but I'd like her a lot more if she didn't have a big silver whistle hanging from her neck. Sometimes she actually blows that whistle and when she does, my small, sensitive ears quiver and quake.

'Mrs Brisbane, there's something very odd happening with some of your students,' she said.

Mrs Brisbane looked surprised. 'What's that?'

'They're talking nonsense and lurching about, waving their arms and – well – something's wrong,' Mrs Wright said.

'Which students?' Mrs Brisbane asked.

'Oh, a lot of them,' Mrs Wright said. 'But not all of them. Whatever is going on, some of your students are being left out.'

'I've noticed some of that behaviour,' Mrs Brisbane said. 'But when I've asked about it, I haven't had a straight answer.'

'Students in the playground need to play proper games,' Mrs Wright said. 'Please get to the bottom of this and stop this behaviour now.'

'I will,' Mrs Brisbane said. 'I definitely will.'

Mrs Wright fingered her whistle and I braced myself.

Luckily, she decided not to blow it, which was a *big* relief to me.

'Class, I need your help,' Mrs Brisbane said when my friends were back from break. 'I want someone to explain why you've been acting strangely lately. I've noticed it and Mrs Wright has noticed it.'

Nobody said a word.

'I've seen some of you doing these odd movements and nodding, waving, muttering nonsense words,' she continued. 'Would someone like to tell me what's going on? How about you, Thomas?'

'I know what you're talking about, but I don't know what they're doing, either. And that's the truth,' he replied.

'I believe you, Thomas,' Mrs Brisbane said.

'How about you, Kelsey?'

Kelsey's face turned almost as red as her bright red hair.

'We're just being silly,' she said.

Mrs Brisbane looked at Tall-Paul. Then she looked at Small-Paul. 'I know you boys will tell me the truth,' she said.

It's hard not to tell the truth when Mrs Brisbane is looking at you like that.

'We have a secret club,' Tall-Paul said. 'It's kind of an Egyptian thing. I think some of the others have clubs, too.'

'It's just for fun,' Small-Paul added. 'We have secret signals and things like that.'

'Do you have a club, Phoebe?' Mrs Brisbane asked.

Phoebe nodded. 'With Kelsey.'

The room had been very quiet up until then, but suddenly I heard someone sniffle.

It was Holly!

Mrs Brisbane grabbed the box of tissues from her desk and hurried to Holly's table. 'Holly, what's wrong?'

'*I'm* not in a secret club,' she said. 'No one asked me.'

No one asked her! I was unsqueakably shocked.

Phoebe and Kelsey looked surprised, too.

'I thought you were in Rosie's club,' Phoebe said.

'I thought you were in Phoebe's club,' Rosie said.

Mrs Brisbane handed Holly a tissue. 'Please raise your hand if you're in a club,' she said.

Everyone's hand went up except for three: Thomas's, Joey's and Holly's.

I wasn't sure whether to raise my paw or not.

I wasn't officially in a club, but I knew most of their secrets.

Joey looked at Thomas. 'I thought you were in the club with Simon and Harry,' he said.

'I thought *you* were,' Thomas said. 'Maybe we should start our own secret club.'

Joey grinned. 'Yes, and we'll invite Holly!'

I saw Holly smile a little bit through her tears.

'That's a nice idea,' Mrs Brisbane said. 'But I have a better idea: Get rid of the secret clubs. Now.'

Someone moaned.

'You see how hurtful it can be to form secret clubs and leave some of your classmates out, don't you?' Mrs Brisbane asked.

'I certainly do!' I shouted.

Even if my friends can't understand me, sometimes I have to squeak up.

Mrs Brisbane paced back and forth in front of the class. 'I can't control what you do outside of this classroom, but from this moment on, there will be nothing to do with secret clubs in Room Twenty-six. Not a signal, not a silly word, not a glance, do you understand me?' she asked.

My friends all nodded and looked terribly sorry.

'Secrets have their place but they have a way of getting out of hand,' Mrs Brisbane explained. 'I know you all like Thomas and Joey and Holly, but you hurt their feelings.'

My friends looked even sorrier.

'I had another lesson planned for now, but first I think we should all play a little game,' she said.

No one seemed to be in the mood for a game, but when Mrs Brisbane told them to put their chairs in a circle, my friends all did.

Mrs Brisbane wrote something on a piece of paper and folded it.

'All right. I've written a secret message on this paper. I'm going to whisper what I wrote in Holly's ear. Then she's going to whisper it to Simon and you'll go all around the circle, whispering the words you hear. You can't ask the person to repeat it. Just pass on what you think you heard.'

She leaned down and whispered in Holly's ear. Holly nodded and turned to whisper in Simon's ear.

Simon looked puzzled. But he couldn't ask Holly to repeat what she'd said, so he whispered in Rosie's ear.

Rosie laughed and then whispered in Felipe's ear.

And so it went, all around the room.

The last person to receive the message was Thomas.

'All right, Thomas,' Mrs Brisbane said. 'Stand up and tell the class the secret message.'

'It doesn't make a lot of sense,' Thomas said. 'But here goes: I think bumpy frogs have a sweet cub, but I want snoring mules.'

For a few seconds, nothing happened.

Then suddenly everyone burst out laughing.

I wasn't laughing, because the message didn't make any sense. Why would Mrs Brisbane whisper that to anyone?

'Thomas, here's the paper with the real message. Please read it,' Mrs Brisbane said.

Thomas stared at it and then he smiled. 'It says, "I think Humphrey and Og have a secret club, but I don't know the rules."'

'We don't have a secret club!' I squeaked, but no one could hear me over all the laughter.

'BOING-BOING-BOING!' Og twanged loudly.

Then Mrs Brisbane called on all the students to say what they'd heard.

'I think jumpy Og has a secret cub, but I want to know mules,' Nicole said.

Sophie had heard, 'I think jumpy Og has a sweet club, but I go to school.'

'Snoring mules' had come from Harry.

And 'jumpy Og' became 'bumpy frog' when Kelsey passed the message along.

It may sound silly, but Og *is* a bit jumpy and

bumpy and he is a frog. But I've never heard of a snoring mule!

'How could the message change like that?' Tall-Paul asked.

'They did it on purpose!' Rosie said.

But Mrs Brisbane said that no one did it on purpose. 'This game shows how when we spread secrets and rumours, the words get fuzzy and the information passed along isn't correct. Unless you *do* want snoring mules.'

She paused while everyone giggled. I giggled a little bit, too.

'I wanted to show you how secrets can get out of hand,' she said. 'I know the last thing anyone wanted to do was to hurt anyone else.'

My friends looked serious again.

Then Slow-Down-Simon raised his hand. 'Mrs Brisbane, can we play the game again?'

And they did.

The day moved so quickly, I was unsqueakably surprised when the final bell rang.

I moved to the front of my cage and squeaked good-bye to everyone.

I was HAPPY-HAPPY-HAPPY to see Holly walk out with Phoebe and Kelsey. And she was *laughing*!

Felipe, Tall-Paul, Small-Paul waited for everyone to leave and then approached our teacher.

'Mrs Brisbane, I know you don't want to hear any more about secret clubs,' Tall-Paul said.

'That's right,' she said.

'But in our club, we made a version of an ancient Egyptian board game called Senet,' Felipe said. 'We thought it would be fun to share with the class.'

Mrs Brisbane smiled. 'I think so, too. Bring it tomorrow. In fact, maybe all the clubs will share their secrets with the rest of the class.'

The Flying Pharaohs looked pleased as they left Room 26.

Mrs Brisbane seemed pleased, too.

'Humphrey and Og, let me tell you something. After all my years of teaching, I can say that there's never a dull day.'

'I know!' I squeaked. 'I've only been here a short time, but I haven't seen a dull day yet!'

Which was true. In fact, I'd never seen a day

where I hadn't learned something new about humans.

Soon, Mrs Brisbane left and the room was quiet again.

It was just getting dark when I saw the door open. It was too early for Aldo to arrive, so who could it be?

For a moment, I was afraid it was the ghost of King Tut!

But as the figure got closer, I saw that it was Ms Mac. In fact, I could smell that it was Ms Mac, who is the best-smelling creature I've ever known.

'Hi, Humphrey and Og,' she said. 'I heard a lot of laughing coming from your room today.'

'They played a silly game!' I told her. 'It was FUN-FUN-FUN!'

'Oh, Humphrey, I've been looking at different pets for my first-graders. I haven't found the perfect one yet. Except for you,' she said. 'And Og.'

'BOING-BOING!' Og thanked her.

'So tell me,' she said. 'If I get another hamster, will your feelings be hurt?'

I was silent for a minute.

On the one paw, I didn't really want Ms Mac to get another hamster. I was afraid I'd feel jealous, the way I felt when Og first came to Room 26.

Jealousy is not a good feeling.

On the other paw, Ms Mac's class deserved to have a classroom pet to teach them about other species and taking care of pets and, well, life.

'I promise, my feelings won't be hurt,' I squeaked.

I had my toes crossed again, because I wasn't sure that was *completely* true. Again.

'Don't tell anyone I said it, but you're the best, Humphrey,' Ms Mac whispered.

I know she meant it.

Humphrey's Top Secret Scribbles

I have a little secret that I mustn't ever
tell,
But I love Ms Mac completely – and her
lovely smell!

11
Secret Whispers

Without all the waving, wiggling, nodding and made-up words from the secret clubs, the work on the Egyptian projects went a lot better.

On Tuesday, Felipe, Tall-Paul and Small-Paul shared their Senet game with the class. It was a rainy day, so my friends stayed inside during break and took turns playing it.

Phoebe and Kelsey brought in their set of hieroglyphs and the Scribes used some of the symbols for the alphabet they were creating.

The only problem I could see was Joey. He was constantly reading *The Jungle Book* when he was supposed to be doing schoolwork.

Still, Mrs Brisbane never said a word.

'Which story do you like best so far?' Thomas

asked Joey before class started

'Ummm.' Joey thought for a minute. 'Mowgli living with the wolves, I guess.'

'Me too,' Thomas said. 'But wait until you get to the part about the tiger!'

That must be some book. I'll have to get my paws on it someday.

'I didn't know a lot of the words,' Joey said. 'But I figured them out by the story.'

Mrs Brisbane joined the conversation. 'It's always fun to talk about a book you liked with someone else who's read it,' she said.

Thomas nodded. 'We should decide what book we're both going to read next so we can talk about it afterwards.'

'Like a book club,' Mrs Brisbane said.

'What's that?' Joey asked.

Mrs Brisbane explained that it's a club where all the people read the same book and then get together to talk about what they liked and didn't like and answer questions.

'That sounds great!' Thomas said.

'We could start a book club right here in Room Twenty-six. We could meet during lunch,' Mrs Brisbane suggested.

'I thought there weren't going to be any more clubs in here,' Thomas said.

Mrs Brisbane smiled. 'No more secret clubs, Thomas. This will be a club anyone can join.'

'Even me?' I squeaked.

'Even Humphrey and Og?' Joey asked.

'Well, they could . . . if they could read,' our teacher answered.

It's unsqueakably frustrating to me that nobody knows that I can read.

I may not know all the words, like Joey, but I can read just fine!

(I'm still not sure about Og, though.)

It was a BUSY-BUSY-BUSY morning in Room 26. First, Mrs Brisbane told my classmates to put the finishing touches on their projects.

There was a lot of last-minute whispering as everyone glued and pasted and drew.

After lunch, the groups presented their finished Egyptian projects. Mrs Brisbane was so proud of their work, she invited Mr Morales and Mr Fitch to join us. Mr Morales even wore a tie with little pyramids on it!

The Traders unveiled their boat first. It was long and tall, with a huge sail, and its ends curved upwards. There were all kinds of interesting things on the boat, such as wood, gold, precious oils and even monkeys. Tall-Paul explained what each thing was and Felipe said where it came from. The places had wonderful names!

All these things would be traded in an open-air market.

Then Holly and Harry acted out how the traders argued over the price.

Harry said something like, 'I will give you a copper jar for that cloth.'

Then Holly folded her arms across her chest, shook her head and said, 'No way. Five copper jars.' She held up five fingers.

No matter what Harry said, Holly would shake her head and say, 'No.'

Harry got so frustrated, he finally said, 'Holly, you're supposed to come down in what you asked! We're supposed to meet in the middle.'

'Do not insult me! This cloth is made of the finest wool! Five copper jars or nothing!' Holly replied.

She was so good, I almost believed she was a trader in ancient Egypt.

Harry didn't know what to do.

'Hurry-Up-Harry,' Tall-Paul said in a loud whisper.

Poor Harry gave in and said, 'Okay, five copper jars. But that wasn't fair!'

Everybody applauded when they finished.

'You all did a great job,' Mr Morales said. 'And Holly, you're quite a performer. Are you heading for Hollywood?'

'Any day now,' Holly said. 'You'll see me on TV. Maybe I'll have my own show.'

My friends all laughed and Holly laughed, too.

The Scribes were next. First, they passed around a piece of papyrus they'd made so everyone could see it (except Og and me).

'Papyrus was made from reeds, which were chopped, peeled and then sliced,' Phoebe explained.

'Then they were pounded into sheets,' Cassie explained.

Thomas spoke next. 'It was really expensive, so only important things were written down.

So I guess teachers didn't give a lot of homework.'

Everybody laughed, including Mrs Brisbane.

'I just made the last part up,' Thomas said.

While Phoebe passed out copies of their hieroglyphs to everyone (except Og and me) and wrote a secret message on the board, Daniel explained that at first, each picture stood for a word.

'Later, symbols began to stand for sounds instead,' he said.

Phoebe's writing didn't look like any message I'd seen before, with pictures of eyes and shapes and swirly things.

Slow-Down-Simon, who was fast at everything, solved it first. '"Being a scribe is the best job in Egypt,"' he shouted.

For a prize, he got his own piece of papyrus.

Mr Morales praised the Scribes and asked if he could keep the hieroglyphs to show his children. Of course, they said yes. Mr Morales is the Most Important Person at Longfellow School.

I expected Sophie, Nicole, Small-Paul and Just-Joey to show off the animal jars they'd been making. But the Artists had an unsqueakably wonderful surprise in store for us.

'We found a book in the library showing the treasures of King Tut's tomb, so we decided to make some of the other things found there,' Small-Paul explained. 'There were so many wonderful things.'

Mr Fitch nodded. 'Those were the first words of the man who opened King Tut's tomb. Someone called to him and asked if he saw anything. And he replied, "Yes, wonderful things."'

'The pyramids were tombs. These objects were put into the tombs to be used in the next life,' Joey said. 'So there were useful things, as well as toys and games.'

Our Artists had made many wonderful things. A golden chair, a board game, a chest covered in jewels. I don't suppose they were real jewels but they looked beautiful.

They'd also made a golden bird, the animal jars and, finally, a golden head of King Tut!

I don't know where they got the gold paint, but they used a *lot* of it.

The Builders were the last to unveil their project – the Great Pyramid of Giza! It looked perfect and they painted it to look like old stone.

But the best part was it actually opened up (it was in two pieces), and inside they'd drawn a map of the chambers.

They told us so many unsqueakably amazing facts about the pyramid. I wish I'd been able to get out my notebook and write them down, but I don't want my friends to find my secret scribblings.

I do remember that it took millions and millions of huge blocks of stone, thousands of men and probably ten years to build it. No one is sure exactly how they managed to do it!

Mr Morales gave a little speech about how proud he was to be at a school with such hard-working students, and Mr Fitch reminded everyone there were lots of books about Egypt in the library.

After they left, Mrs Brisbane let the students wander around and look closely at each project.

After school, Mrs Wright came in again to talk to Mrs Brisbane.

I shivered a little when I saw the silver whistle. I wonder if she wears it when she sleeps or has a bath.

The thought of having a bath – or getting wet at all – made me quiver, so I concentrated on what she was saying.

'I'm glad to see your students are behaving normally again,' she said. 'Good work. But I have something else to discuss with you.'

'Very well,' Mrs Brisbane said.

'As you know, I'm chairman of the rules committee here,' Mrs Wright began.

Mrs Brisbane nodded.

'I think I should have been consulted about your upcoming event,' Mrs Wright continued. 'There are several issues that concern me.'

'Listen closely, Og! We might find out who's leaving,' I squeaked.

Og quietly splashed in his tank.

'First, all visitors must have passes in advance and I'd like a complete list of who will be here,' Mrs Wright said.

Mrs Brisbane nodded again.

'And I've heard that there will be newspaper and TV reporters and photographers here. I'm afraid that's a problem,' Mrs Wright said.

'But it's such a wonderful story,' Mrs Brisbane said.

'We'd have to have a release form signed by parents of each and every student in your class,' Mrs Wright said. 'No exceptions.'

Mrs Brisbane nodded. 'Yes, I already have them. And the list of people coming.'

She walked to her desk and picked up a folder. 'Here,' she said. 'You can make copies.'

Mrs Wright seemed surprised. 'Oh. Well.'

She carefully looked at each form, which took a while. 'They seem to be in order. But I also heard you'll have balloons,' she said.

'Yes,' Mrs Brisbane said. 'And flowers and maybe even some gifts.'

Mrs Wright frowned. 'I'm not sure you can have balloons and flowers. There are allergies and, well, other things.'

'I'm sure they'll be fine. But if you find anything in the rules that says I can't have them, please let me know,' Mrs Brisbane replied.

By the little smile on her face, I could tell

that Mrs Brisbane already knew those things weren't against the rules.

I was happy when they both finally left for the day because I had a Plan for how I'd spend the evening.

I knew I had time before Aldo came in to clean, so I got out my notebook and pencil and added some new thoughts about the secret of a student leaving Room 26.

Question: Why is Mrs Brisbane happy?
Because I am NOT-NOT-NOT.

- Today, Holly said she might go to Hollywood and have her own television show. She said, 'Any day now.' She is a good actress. Now, that would be a news story!

'Oh, no! Holly is leaving Room Twenty-six!' I said.

I jiggled my lock and raced over to Og's tank, notebook in paw.

'It's Holly that's leaving! I figured it out,' I squeaked.

Then I read him what I wrote in my notebook.

'BOING-BOING-BOING-BOING!' Og said as he jumped up and down.

I guess he liked Holly as much as I did.

'She's always trying to help her friends,' I said. 'Sometimes she goes overboard, but at least she tries! And sometimes when she cries, I want to hug her.'

'BOING!' Og agreed.

'Of course, it will be nice to say we know a famous actress but . . .' I couldn't finish the sentence. I guess I felt a little bit like crying myself, but I don't know how!

I was so busy feeling sad, I didn't notice that it was dark outside.

Suddenly, I heard the THUMP-THUMP-THUMP of Aldo's cleaning trolley. Then the RATTLE-RATTLE-RATTLE as he turned the doorknob.

'Eeek!' As I raced back to my cage, my notebook flew out of my paws and slid across the table.

Dropping my notebook was a bad thing, but getting caught outside my cage could be worse.

Hopefully I could get it later, so I pulled the cage door behind me, just as the lights came on.

'Never fear, 'cause Aldo's here!' his voice boomed out.

What a close call! My heart was pounding.

At least Aldo hadn't caught me out of my cage and discovered my secret. He would fix my lock-that-doesn't-lock and I'd be stuck in my cage forever!

I looked to see where my notebook ended up and it wasn't on the table! It was on the floor, near the leg of one of the tables. The notebook that's my *biggest* secret!

'Og! My notebook's on the floor!' I squeaked at the top of my small lungs.

'SCREEE!' Og yelled. That's the sound he makes when he thinks there's real danger.

There was danger, all right, but there wasn't one thing I could do except hope that Aldo wouldn't notice the notebook. Or, if he did, he would at least put it somewhere I could get it after he left.

However, Aldo is a GREAT-GREAT-GREAT cleaner, and he doesn't leave much behind.

I watched his every move. He dusted, he picked up rubbish. Then he got out his big broom – the one he can actually balance on one finger – and began to sweep.

My tail was twitching as the broom got closer and closer to my little notebook.

'Fellows, you know that big news I've been talking about?' he said. 'Well, tonight I might tell you.'

Aldo looked over at Og and me but he kept on sweeping. He didn't even notice that the big broom covered my little notebook as he swept everything on the floor into a big pile.

'Maria said it's okay to tell everybody tomorrow, but I can't hold it in another minute,' he said.

He got his big dustpan from the trolley and swept the pile of rubbish – and my notebook – right into it.

'You see, we're not having a baby,' he said. 'We're having *two* babies. Twins!'

'Eeek!' I squeaked.

I wasn't squeaking about the twins. I was squeaking because he dumped the rubbish into the plastic bag in the big bin on his trolley.

'BOING-BOING-BOING!' Og twanged excitedly.

Aldo was so wrapped up in thinking about the twins, he never even noticed!

I felt as if my heart had sunk to the bottom of my toes.

But I managed to squeak, 'Congratulations, Aldo! That's wonderful news.'

'I need to finish college fast so I can get a better job,' he continued. 'I'll have a lot of mouths to feed.'

He mopped the floor but all I could think of was that bag of rubbish.

Finally, it was time for him to eat his dinner, which he always did in Room 26.

As he munched on his sandwich, Aldo talked happily about the twins and becoming a dad. I tried to listen, but my mind was on my notebook.

'I know it's not easy to be a dad,' he said. 'But what's it like to be a double dad?'

I had no idea!

Just then, Aldo's phone rang.

'Maria!' he answered with a smile. Then suddenly he wasn't smiling.

'I'll be right there,' he said. 'I'll just drop off my trolley in my room and be there right away. Stay calm!'

Aldo didn't seem very calm.

'Maria's got a flat tyre,' he said. 'I've got to go and help her.'

In a flash, Aldo tied up the bag of rubbish and pushed the trolley out of the room.

'See you tomorrow!' he said.

I wasn't thinking about tomorrow.

I was thinking about tonight . . . and how I could get my notebook back.

There would be no more secret scribbling until I did.

Secret Mission

As soon as Aldo's car pulled out of the car park, I opened the lock-that-doesn't-lock and hurried over to squeak to Og.

'I'm REALLY-REALLY-REALLY sorry about Maria's flat tyre,' I said. 'But at least I know he was dropping the trolley off in the utility room. And my notebook is in the rubbish bag that's on his trolley.'

'BOING-BOING-BOING!' Og hopped up and down.

I was already racing across the table. 'Wish me luck!'

'BOING-BOING!' Og answered.

I slid down the leg of our table, scampered across the room and squeezed under the door.

I scurried down the hall, past more and more classrooms. Even though I'd never been in Aldo's room, I knew where it was.

After passing Mr Morales's office, I turned the next corner, raced past a drinking fountain, and saw a door with a sign on it: 'Caretaker'.

I hunkered down and slid under the door – OOF!

It was dark inside and there weren't any windows.

There were some glowing lights along the wall where things were plugged in, such as a telephone and a huge torch.

Although I couldn't see much, I knew I was in the right place because I could smell Aldo's trolley.

As a hamster, I have a wonderful sense of smell. My human friends would be surprised to know that each of them has a different smell. I can tell who's standing by my cage with my eyes closed!

I moved forward and there it was – Aldo's trolley with the rubbish bag from Room 26!

I moved closer and gave it a good sniff.

Ah, yes! There was the unmistakable odour

of paint and glue.

The Artists had used a lot of paint on their treasures. And the Builders had used a lot of glue on the pyramid.

I sniffed some more.

There was another familiar smell. Very old bedding. And, yes, my poo!

Do-It-Now-Daniel had cleaned out my cage that day. At the time, I was glad my cage was cleaned, but I wasn't so glad when I thought I might have to dig through my poo!

But I had to keep going.

I didn't want to end up buried in a mountain of rubbish, so I had a Plan. If I didn't have a Plan before trying something so risky, I could be one sorry hamster!

Luckily, the bag was on the bottom shelf.

I gave the corner a swipe with my paw.

It opened a tiny bit, but nothing came out.

So I swiped it a little higher and then a bit more.

The paint and glue smells were getting stronger.

Oh, and so was the poo.

I grabbed one side of the opening with both

paws and tugged with all my might.

Then I ran away as fast as I could because I thought that the whole side of the bag might open.

And I was right!

EEEK! With a gigantic WHOOSH, the rubbish tumbled out like an avalanche!

It really was a mountain of rubbish. And a little bit of poo.

I suddenly wished that I had Og with me to warn me of the time. It could take all night to find my notebook and I didn't want to get caught out of my cage.

It was still hard to see things, so I used my sense of smell and my sense of touch to examine everything there.

Used tissues (*ewww*), bits of pencils and rubbers, paper with glue on it, paper with gold paint on it, a few bits of food. (Who was eating in class?)

Little by little, I climbed the mountain of rubbish, which was not an easy thing to do because things kept shifting under my paws.

UP-UP-UP I went, higher and higher, over mounds of paper, rubber bands, tiny pieces of chalk and markers that had run out of ink. (Markers are very slippery when you're climbing.)

Of course, it would be near the top, since Aldo had swept it up last.

I could almost see the top of the mountain when I felt something flat and firm under my paws.

Something like . . . my notebook!

I didn't have to look at it to know. It was the right size and the right smell.

'Oh, notebook,' I whispered. 'Hello.' I picked it up with my front paws and hugged it close to me.

But I couldn't walk down the mountain on my back legs alone.

I tried holding it with my teeth, but it was heavier than I thought. It made me a little wobbly.

I was trying to work out what to do when my back legs began to quiver and shiver and wobble and – there I went, tumbling down the mountain with my notebook in my teeth.

THUMP! BUMP! SMACK! WHACK! OW! WOW!

I rolled all the way to the bottom – but I still had my notebook!

My Plan had worked, although I hadn't figured in the falling and rolling part.

I was happy. I was relieved. I was tired. But I had to get the notebook back to Room 26.

I was even more tired after pushing the notebook under the door. It was thicker than I was when I squished down my body. I had to use all my strength to force it through.

Slipping myself back under the door wasn't easy, either.

I started my journey back to Room 26 with the notebook in my mouth, but after a while, it felt too heavy.

I placed it on the floor and hopped on top, hoping it would slide like a skateboard, but it didn't budge.

Finally, I gave it a good shove with my front paws.

It moved forward a few inches and so that's what I did for the rest of the night.

Inch by inch, past the office.

Inch by inch, past classroom after classroom.

It was definitely morning when I pushed the

notebook under the door to Room 26, then pushed myself as well.

'I did it, Og! I found the notebook!' I shouted.

'BOING-BOING-BOING-BOING-BOING!'

Even from across the room, I could see that Og was jumping so high, he was about to pop the top of his tank.

'I'll hurry,' I said.

I pushed the notebook across the floor until I reached the table. Then, holding the notebook in my mouth, I grabbed on to the blinds' cord and swung myself UP-UP-UP – which took a lot longer with the extra weight of the notebook.

I leaped on to the table, raced past Og's tank and went into my cage.

At last, I slammed the door behind me and tucked my notebook behind the mirror.

'Home sweet home,' I said.

And I fell asleep.

I try to be a good student and keep up with the lessons in Room 26, but I have to admit that I slept through the whole day.

At the end of the day, I woke up feeling like a brand-new hamster.

In fact, the first thing I did was hop on my wheel and go for a good spin, followed by a big gulp of water, and a tasty snack of mealworms.

Then I settled into my soft bedding and listened to Og splashing around in the water side of his tank.

I guess I dozed off again, but I woke up when Aldo turned on the lights.

I hadn't even heard the RATTLE-RATTLE-RATTLE of his trolley!

'Whooo, boys, I'm sorry I'm late. What a night!' Aldo pulled his trolley into the room.

'What happened?' I squeaked.

Aldo mumbled to himself as he dusted the tables.

'The things I have to do,' he said.

'BOING-BOING!' Og replied.

'If I could get my hands on that rotten rodent . . .' he muttered.

'Eeek!' I squeaked. I was one worried rodent.

Aldo waved his dusting cloth. 'You won't believe what happened!' I'd never seen Aldo look so angry. 'I was in such a hurry to help Maria change the tyre, I put the trolley with the rubbish bag in my room.'

(I already knew that.)

Aldo continued. 'Last night, some critter – it must have been a mouse – got into my room and chewed through the bin bag. When I went in there this evening, there was a mountain of rubbish all over the floor!'

Ooops!

'I had to spend an extra half an hour getting it all back in the bag and cleaning the floor,' Aldo said.

'BOING-BOING!' Og twanged.

I was sorry, too.

Aldo shook his head. 'I hate to do it, but I'm going to have to set some mousetraps. So if you smell cheese, Humphrey, don't go for it. I'd hate to see you get trapped.'

'EEEK-EEEK-EEEK!' I squeaked. Traps! I thought I might faint.

'I keep this place so clean, we've never had a mouse in Longfellow School before,' Aldo said.

'It's not your fault,' I murmured. 'It's my fault.'

For once, I was glad he couldn't understand me.

Aldo sighed. 'I was pretty cross tonight, but then I thought about the twins and I felt better. But I have to finish school – fast!'

'You can do it!' I squeaked.

After Aldo left, I thought about the mousetrap. But then I remembered that there wasn't actually a mouse after all. There was only me.

That piece of cheese would not be touched.

I was unsqueakably sorry that I was the cause of Aldo's extra work.

And I vowed to take better care of my notebook.

Humphrey's Top Secret Scribbles

I'm HAPPY-HAPPY-HAPPY to have my
notebook back to stay.
And I HOPE-HOPE-HOPE it will never
go away.

No More Secrets

For a while, school was back to normal.

Mrs Brisbane taught and the students worked. And learned. And had some fun.

I went home with Rolling-Rosie for the weekend and had FUN-FUN-FUN showing her all my tricks.

At the beginning of the next week, Mrs Brisbane made an announcement. 'Class, we're starting a new club in Room Twenty-six, but it won't be secret,' she said. 'It's a Book Club, where we all read a book and discuss it. Holly, would you hand out these information sheets to send home to the parents? Read it, discuss it and, if you're interested, you can sign up.'

The Book Club sounded pawsitively wonderful.

But when I saw Helpful-Holly handing out the papers, I felt a pang.

Soon, she'd be moving to Hollywood and I'd never see her again, unless I saw her on TV.

Who would Mrs Brisbane call on for help?

And how would we feel without her around? How would I feel?

I saw Thomas and Joey give each other a thumbs-up. They looked happy about the book club, but they didn't know Holly was moving away.

When was she going to go?

On Tuesday morning, I found out when Holly was leaving.

Mr Morales came into the classroom before school to talk to Mrs Brisbane. He had on a tie with tiny flags on it.

'Here's the revised schedule,' he said. 'So . . . at ten o'clock you can expect some special visitors. As you can see, the TV reporter Sandy Starr will be doing an intro in the hallway beforehand. Then they'll film in the classroom and do some interviews.'

Mrs Brisbane smiled. *Smiled!* 'This will be a day to remember.'

The day Holly was leaving felt like a day I'd like to forget.

'Did you give the schedule to Mrs Wright?' Mrs Brisbane asked.

'Oh, yes,' Mr Morales said. 'I don't want to get in trouble.'

It was FUNNY-FUNNY-FUNNY to think that Mr Morales, who is the head, didn't want to get in trouble with Mrs Wright, who is a teacher.

Maybe he was afraid of her whistle, too.

I hopped on my wheel and did some spinning to help me calm down a bit.

Og splashed around in his tank. Maybe he needed calming down, too.

My friends all came into class, laughing and talking.

Holly showed Rosie the book she was reading and I heard them talk about joining the book club.

But Holly wouldn't be joining the book club.

Do they have book clubs in Hollywood? And isn't it funny that a girl named Holly was moving to a place called Hollywood?

I watched the hand on the clock inch its way from 8.00 to 8.30 to 9.00 to 9.30.

My friends went out for break, and I spun on my wheel some more.

By the time my classmates were back in their seats, the clock had inched its way to 9.55.

Five minutes until the surprise!

At 10.00, Mrs Brisbane was talking about the book club again when there was a knock at the door. She acted surprised.

'I wonder who that could be?' she said.

As if she didn't know.

She walked over and opened the door. 'Well, it looks like we have some special visitors!'

A man and a woman – both wearing uniforms – entered. The woman carried a huge teddy bear. The man had a big bunch of balloons.

I knew that woman – it was Phoebe's mum.

The man must be Phoebe's dad.

When I glanced over at Phoebe, she looked as shocked and surprised as I was!

'Phoebe . . . we're home!' her mum said.

'We're all going to be together again,' her dad said.

Phoebe raced over to her parents and the three of them hugged and hugged and hugged some more.

'You're here! You're really home!' Phoebe cried.

My friends were buzzing with excitement.

Calm-Down-Cassie was so excited she got up and started jumping up and down and clapping.

Og splashed around like crazy and I let out a loud 'Yippee!'

Phoebe's grandmother had come in, too, along with people with cameras and a perky woman with a microphone who must have been Sandy Starr!

So many cameras flashed, all I could see were coloured dots floating in front of my eyes.

When she had finished hugging her parents, Phoebe hugged her grandmother.

Then Sandy Starr moved in with her microphone. 'Phoebe, how does it feel to see your parents again?' she asked.

I was pretty sure I already knew the answer to that.

'Oh, I'm so happy!' Phoebe's voice quivered as they hugged her again. 'It's just what I wished for.'

'Are you home to stay?' the reporter asked Phoebe's parents.

'Yes,' her dad said. 'We're all moving back to Winfield.'

For the first time, I looked at my other classmates. Some of them looked happy and some looked surprised. Kelsey was actually crying.

Mr Morales and Mrs Wright came into the classroom to shake hands with Phoebe and her parents.

Phoebe hugged her grandmother again. 'You didn't tell me!' she said. 'Oh, but I'll miss you.'

'Don't you worry,' her grandmother said. 'I'm coming to visit you a *lot*!'

Sandy Starr asked Phoebe and her parents a lot of questions. She interviewed Mrs Brisbane and Mr Morales, and then went to talk to some of the other students.

'How do you feel about Phoebe's good news?' she asked Tell-the-Truth-Thomas.

He looked surprised to have a camera in his

face, but he smiled and said, 'I'm happy for her. But I'll miss her.'

Sandy Starr turned to Holly. 'Were you surprised by what happened today?'

Holly looked directly at the camera. 'Yes, I was,' she said. 'I'll miss Phoebe so much, but I know she'll be happy to be with her parents again.'

It looked like Holly was going to be on TV after all!

Then the man with the TV camera said he wanted to get some shots of our room. So he moved all around, filming my friends, Mrs Brisbane and he even brought his camera over to our table.

'HI-HI-HI!' I squeaked as he passed by. Everything happened so fast, I could hardly keep up. Then suddenly, all the cameras and guests – and even Phoebe – were gone.

'Class, I know this day has been an exciting roller coaster,' Mrs Brisbane said. 'Let's talk about it.'

'YES-YES-YES!' I squeaked, which made everyone laugh.

I've always known that Mrs Brisbane was a

great teacher, but that day, I knew it even more.

She talked to my friends about how difficult it had been for Phoebe to be so far away from her parents. But her parents had an important job to do for the country.

'Don't forget, lots of children have parents serving in the armed forces,' she said.

Then she talked about how Phoebe's grandmother had helped her deal with her loneliness and her worries about her parents. And she told my fellow classmates that their friendship with Phoebe had been a big help to her whole family.

'We'll all miss Phoebe,' she said in a shaky voice. 'But we have to be happy for her.'

My whiskers wilted and my tail twitched.

I felt as sad as I had when Ms Mac left and went FAR-FAR-FAR away.

But I had to be happy for Phoebe.

The next morning, Phoebe came to school as usual.

Once class began, Mrs Brisbane asked her if she had anything to say to her friends.

'Today is my last day in Room Twenty-six,' she said. 'I'll miss you all so much, but I'm so happy to be with my mum and dad. But we can keep in touch – please?'

My friends all said they'd keep in touch, but I didn't know how I could do that.

At the end of the day, when her parents came to pick her up, Phoebe came over to the table where Og and I live.

'Humphrey and Og, I know I've sometimes been forgetful this year,' she said. 'I was always thinking about my parents. But I want you both to know that I'll never, ever forget either one of you.'

Then she gave me a little piece of carrot and she threw some Froggy Fish Sticks into Og's tank.

'BOING-BOING-BOING!' Og thanked her as he dived for the food.

'Thanks, Phoebe,' I squeaked. 'I love you.'

I know she couldn't understand me, but for some reason she said, 'I love you, too, Humphrey.'

Room 26 was very quiet on Thursday.

Mrs Brisbane announced the first book for the Book Club – it was set in Egypt!

I could tell that Kelsey especially missed Phoebe. After all, they'd been Sisters of the Nile. But the other girls spent more time with her and by the end of the day, she even smiled a little bit.

I spent a lot of time spinning on my wheel.

I was HAPPY-HAPPY-HAPPY that Phoebe was with her parents. I'd heard her say how much she missed them.

But I was SAD-SAD-SAD to lose a friend.

I was cheered up quite a bit when Tall-Paul stopped by my cage before school one day.

'Guess what, Humphrey? My parents are getting me a hamster!' He had a huge smile on his face. 'You convinced them and they kept it a secret all this time! I'm getting it this week-end. Thanks!'

'You're welcome,' I said.

It would be nice to be a pet for just one child. But I think it's even better to be the pet of a whole class.

After school, I was about to grab my notebook and write down my thoughts, when the door opened and Ms Mac came in.

'Hi, Humphrey,' she said. 'You had a big week. It was great to see you on TV the other night.'

I had been on TV, too!

'I'm sure you miss Phoebe, the way I missed you when I left Room Twenty-six and went to Brazil.'

'I was SAD-SAD-SAD!!!' I squeaked.

'I told you how I've missed having a classroom pet,' she said.

I don't know why, but her voice sounded . . . different.

'So, I finally made a decision and got a pet for Room Twelve. Not a hamster, of course,' she said. 'No hamster could ever be as wonderful as you are. So I got . . . a guinea pig!'

'Eeek!' I shouted.

'BOING-BOING!' Og yelled.

'Calm down,' she said with a smile. 'I'm only thinking of my students. As you know, you can learn a lot about yourself by taking care of another species.'

That was something Ms Mac told me when she first brought me to Room 26. And I've tried hard to be the best classroom pet I could.

'Gigi is a very nice guinea pig,' she said. 'I'll take you in to meet her sometime. Maybe you can give her some tips.'

Gigi? A *her*?

'I'll try,' I said, even though my heart was hurting a tiny bit.

Ms Mac glanced at her watch. 'The bad news is, I've got to go and meet a friend across town. I can't leave Gigi in the car, so she's going to have to spend the night in my classroom,' she said. 'Just like you did when I left.'

It was lonely without Ms Mac and it didn't help that my heart was broken.

She got up to leave, but she turned back.

'I almost forgot,' she said. 'I brought you a little present. I thought it might be time for a new one.'

Without another word, she opened my cage and stuck a brand-new tiny notebook behind my mirror.

And she left.

I sat and thought.

The room grew dark and I thought some more.

'Og, did I ever tell you that my first night alone here in Room Twenty-six was unsqueakably scary?' I asked my neighbour.

'BOING!' Og seemed surprised.

'That was before you came,' I said. 'And I had no idea what a classroom pet does.'

Og dived into the water side of his tank.

'Gigi probably doesn't know the first thing about being a classroom pet, either,' I said.

Og splashed loudly in his tank.

Soon I heard the RATTLE-RATTLE-RATTLE of Aldo's cleaning trolley, and the lights came on.

'Hello, my friends,' Aldo said as he entered Room 26 wearing a big smile. 'I have good news! There were no mice in the traps. And nobody got into my rubbish bags. So maybe the problem is solved.'

I was as relieved as Aldo was about the mice.

As far as I was concerned, he would NEVER-EVER-EVER find a broken rubbish bag again!

After he left, the room was dark again. I heard the loud ticking of the clock.

I remember how that sound scared me on my first night in Room 26.

I opened the lock-that-doesn't-lock and hurried across the table. 'Og, maybe I should at least say hello to Gigi. She must be feeling a little lonely,' I said. 'I'll give her your regards.'

'BOING-BOING!' It sounded as if Og agreed.

So I slid down the leg of our table, as I have done so many times before, and scampered to Room 12. When I got there, the room was so dark I couldn't see a thing.

But I could smell a brand-new smell.

Gigi.

'Gigi?' I squeaked. 'Don't be afraid. I'm your friend. My name is Humphrey and I'm one of the classroom pets in Room Twenty-six. We also have a frog named Og. He told me to say "Hi" from him, too. Oh, and I'm a friend of Ms Mac's.'

I heard a very soft 'Squeak, squeak.'

And I knew that meant 'Hi, Humphrey.'

I never knew I spoke Guinea Pig!

I moved a little closer and saw a dark figure huddled in the corner of a cage. I think Gigi was shaking.

'You're unsqueakably lucky to be a classroom pet – especially in Ms Mac's class,' I told her. 'And you'll have a wonderful time with your classmates. I hope you get to go home with them at the weekends. They'll have problems you'll help them solve and you'll work hard.'

Gigi squeaked again.

'In the end, you'll have the best time a hamster or guinea pig ever had. And you know what – you'll make a difference,' I told her.

By then, my eyes had adjusted to the light and I could see Gigi. She was quite a bit larger than I am. And I saw that she'd stopped shaking. But she was still in the corner.

'I'm going back to Room Twenty-six now, but I'll come visit you again some night, and if you have any questions, I might be able to give you some tips,' I said.

'Thanks,' Gigi said in a soft voice.

I was almost to the door when I remembered something.

I turned back towards Gigi's cage. 'Oh, and you might want to try jiggling the lock on your cage,' I said. 'Just in case you have a lock-that-doesn't-lock, too.'

Who knows? She might have big adventures outside her cage like me.

Humphrey's Top Secret Scribbles

Friendships like Phoebe's never-ever end. But there's always room for a brand-new friend.

Humphrey's Tips about Keeping and Telling Secrets

1. Some secrets are okay, such as a surprise party that everybody knows about except the guest of honour. And that person will find out anyway! Surprise!

2. If you're planning a gift for someone, it's FINE-FINE-FINE to keep it a secret. It won't be a secret for ever, and it's something nice.

3. Secrets that make you feel bad or scared or bother you are NOT good to keep and you should tell somebody, like a parent or a teacher.

4. Secrets that leave others out – and hurt people's feelings – are definitely not good. Don't do that! You wouldn't like that!

5. Hurtful gossip – which means bad things people say about others behind their backs – should not be shared with others, unless it's something that scares or worries you. Then, tell a grown-up.

6. Secret notebooks are fine, but sometimes they get found by the wrong person, so don't write anything you wouldn't want someone else to see.

7. Secrets that make you not safe aren't good to keep.

8. Secret locks-that-don't-lock aren't a good idea, unless you're an adventurous hamster!

9. If you accidentally find out someone else's happy secret, keep it to yourself. Let the person with the secret share it at the right time.

10. Here's the thing: Tell an adult about any secret (or anything else) that bothers you and don't do anything to make someone else feel bad. That's it!